The Trail to Santa Fe

BY DAVID LAVENDER

Illustrated by Nicholas Eggenhofer

TRAILS WEST PUBLISHING
Santa Fe, New Mexico

TRAILS WEST PUBLISHING
PO Box 8619, Santa Fe, New Mexico 87504-8619

1 9 8 9

Trails West edition
design by Lucy Jelinek

For Newton Chase

The Trail to Santa Fe

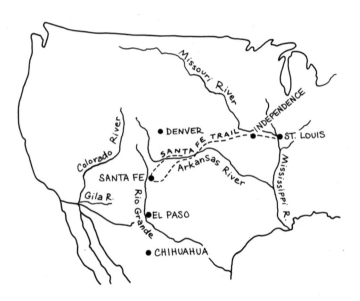

TABLE OF CONTENTS

INTRODUCTION 9

SANTA FE TRAIL DATES 11

MYSTERIOUS SPANISH LANDS 15

FORBIDDEN CITY 24

TRAIL BLAZERS 30

TRIBESMEN AND TRADERS CLASH 39

CARAVANS ROLL 46

BIGGEST TRADING POST IN THE WEST 55

BEYOND SANTA FE 63

RAIDERS FROM TEXAS 70

ARMY ON THE TRAIL 78

TRAGIC YEARS 85

STEEL WHEELS ROLL 93

A FEW MORE BOOKS TO READ 103

INDEX 107

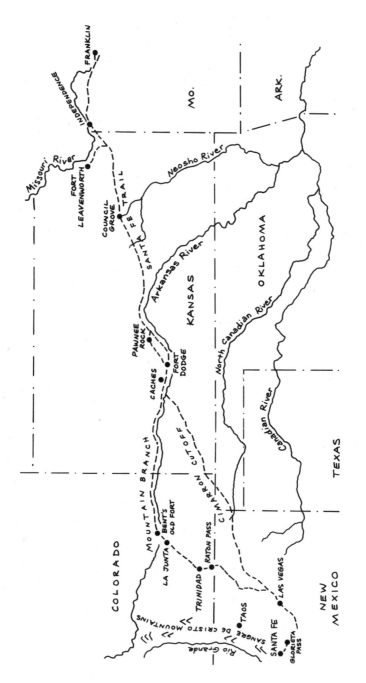

The Trail to Santa Fe

INTRODUCTION

On a January day in 1822 William Becknell halted his horse on a dirt street in the frontier village of Franklin, Missouri and called out to passersby. In one hand he held a bulging leather sack, in the other a hunting knife. As onlookers gathered, Becknell raised the sack high above his head and with a flash of sharp steel slit the leather. Mexican pesos rained down. The silver coins rang and glittered as they rolled into the stone-lined gutters bordering the narrow street.

The townspeople hastened closer to hear Becknell's tale of the nearly two thousand mile ride he had just finished and of the riches that were to be made in trade with faraway Santa Fe. Mexico had won independence from Spain, he explained, and the once-forbidden city of Santa Fe was open to commerce with Americans.

When the new grass was up the following spring Becknell and twenty-one other daring merchants loaded three wagons with goods and set out to return to New Mexico. The Santa Fe Trail was born! For nearly sixty years wagon trains would groan back and forth across the Trail carrying travelers to adventure and enterprise. Some travelers found fame and riches on the Santa Fe Trail, others only hardship and an early death.

On a February day in 1880 a steam locomotive puffed into Santa Fe. Steel rails now connected New Mexico with the rest of the United States. Wagon trains became a thing of the past, and the Santa Fe Trail faded into history.

But the Trail didn't disappear. It left its mark upon the land. At many places along the old trace between Missouri and New Mexico ruts cut by the wagon wheels are visible to this day. Landmarks used by wagonmasters to guide their route remain for modern travelers to see as well. And the Santa Fe Trail left its mark upon the people. The story of the hardship and adventure encountered by the old travelers, and the courage and determination with which they faced all obstacles, continues to stir the hearts of all who take the time to learn about the Trail.

Today several National Memorials, Monuments and Historic Sites commemorate the Santa Fe Trail, along with numerous state parks and monuments. In 1987 President Ronald Reagan signed legislation making the Santa Fe Trail a National Historic Trail. The National Park Service began surveying the entire trail route to identify and preserve for modern travelers all that remains of this great historic highway.

David Lavender is the perfect guide to lead modern readers — young and old — through the colorful history of the Santa Fe Trail. Born high in the San Juan Mountains in Telluride, Colorado, he has spent most of his life studying and writing about the history of the American West. He has authored more than twenty-five books including WESTWARD VISION: THE STORY OF THE OREGON TRAIL; THE FIST IN THE WILDERNESS, a history of the fur trade; BENTS FORT; and two books in the Regions of America series: THE ROCKIES and THE SOUTHWEST.

SANTA FE TRAIL DATES

1806   Lieutenant Zebulin Pike led his party west from St. Louis in July to explore the route to the Rocky Mountains.

1807   In March Lt. Pike and his command arrived in Santa Fe as prisoners of the Spanish.

1807-   Santa Fe remained closed to all foreign merchants.
1821

1821   In September Mexico won independence from Spain.
In November William Becknell led the first party of traders into Santa Fe.

1822   William Becknell and associates returned to Santa Fe using wagons for the first time to haul merchandise across the prairies.

1824   The first full-scale merchant caravan journeyed to Santa Fe.

1825   The United States Government surveyed a route from Missouri to Santa Fe but the traders never used the Government's route.

1828   McNees and Munroe were killed by Indians. The traders' retaliation touched off a series of clashes between traders and Indians.

1829   United States soldiers accompanied the spring caravan. Their supply wagons were pulled by oxen.

Charles and William Bent entered the Santa Fe trade. The starting point of the Santa Fe Trail was moved from Franklin, Missouri to Independence.

1830   Jedediah Smith was killed on the Trail.

1833   Bent's Fort was built. It became the most famous landmark in the Southwest.

1841   The ill-fated Texas-Santa Fe expedition set out to invade New Mexico.

1842- Raiders from Texas attempted to disrupt Santa Fe Trail traffic.

1843 Antonio José Chávez was murdered by raiders from Texas.

1846 The United States declared war on Mexico.
Colonel Stephen Watts Kearny led the Army of the West to Santa Fe.
New Mexico claimed as United States territory.

1847 Residents of Taos rebelled against United States rule.
Territorial Governor Charles Bent was killed.

1849 William Bent blew up Bent's Fort and built Bent's New Fort at the Big Timbers.
Gold seekers traveled the Santa Fe Trail en route to California.

1862 Confederate invaders were defeated at the battle of Glorieta Pass on the Santa Fe Trail.

1865 The Kansas Pacific Railroad started toward Denver, Colorado.
The eastern end of the Santa Fe Trail moved west with the railroad.

1873 The Atchison, Topeka and Santa Fe Railroad reached the Colorado border.

1879 The Atchison, Topeka and Santa Fe Railroad crossed Raton Pass into New Mexico.

1880 The Atchison, Topeka and Santa Fe Railroad reached Santa Fe on February 16.

1987 The Santa Fe Trail was declared a National Historic Trail.

1

Mysterious Spanish Lands

*U*naware that secret agents of Spain were watching every step he took, young Lieutenant Zebulon Montgomery Pike hurried among the stores and warehouses of St. Louis, making purchases of camp equipment. His eyes shone, for he had just received dazzling orders. From the entire Army of the United States, he had been selected to lead an exploring expedition across the unknown plains of the Midwest to the far-off Rocky Mountains. And he was only twenty-seven years old!

Success on his mission would mean a great boost forward to Pike's career. It might prove equally important to his country. Three years before, in 1803, the infant United States had doubled its size by purchasing from France the huge wilderness known as Louisiana. Excepting Texas, whose boundaries in those days stretched even farther than they do now, Louisiana included the entire region between the Mississippi River and the Rocky Mountains.

What riches and what dangers lay inside that vast area? The United States Government was eager to learn. In 1804, Lewis and Clark had been sent across Louisiana's northern reaches to the Pacific Ocean.

Pike himself during the summer of 1805 had explored northward along the headwaters of the Mississippi. Now this even more important mission awaited him — a venture across the central plains toward the boundaries of the mysterious Spanish province of New Mexico.

To accomplish his bold journey of nearly a thousand miles Pike was given a command of only twenty soldiers. At the last minute the group was joined by a civilian doctor named John Robinson.

Considerable mystery surrounded John Robinson. On the face of things he was making the difficult trip simply to do an errand for a friend of his, a merchant in Illinois. Some years earlier this merchant had hired a man named LaLande to take some trade goods among the Indians of the plains. LaLande had vanished with the goods, and there was reason to think he had gone to Santa Fe. The merchant wanted to recover his losses, and when he heard of Pike's expedition, he asked that Dr. Robinson be allowed to accompany the troops as far as the border of New Mexico. From the border Robinson might be able to continue alone to Santa Fe and collect the money due on the lost goods.

Surprisingly, the Army agreed — and not just so that Robinson could overtake a thief. General Wilkinson, Commander of the Army, wanted information about the resources and strength of his government's new neighbor in the Southwest. American troops, however, could not legally march onto the soil of New Mexico. But as a private citizen bound on an honorable errand, Dr. Robinson might be allowed to reach Santa Fe. On the way, he could use his eyes. The doctor was, in short, a spy.

Robinson was running a grave risk. Spain's policy in those days was to be secretive and jealous about her possessions in North America. The few French traders who had managed to reach Santa Fe from the Mississippi Valley in the early days before the Louisiana Purchase had been promptly ordered back home. Americans could expect even more severe treatment, for in the early 1800's dangerous tension existed between Spain and the United States.

The Spanish feared the Americans. Ever since the United States had won its freedom from England in the Revolution, restless pioneers had been swarming in increasing numbers across the Allegheny

Mountains. If Pike's expedition succeeded in finding an easy route to Santa Fe, footloose adventurers would follow it to the very gates of New Mexico. Would the Americans be content to stop there? Might they not want their possessions extended on beyond the mountains to California and the shores of the Pacific?

Thus, though the Spanish agents in St. Louis may not have known that Robinson was a spy, they were instantly suspicious of Pike's whole expedition. Almost the minute the young lieutenant began his preparations, word of what he was doing was rushed to Mexico. From there emissaries hurried orders north to Santa Fe. The Americans must not be allowed to come too near!

Quickly a Mexican force was fitted out to turn Pike back. It consisted of 600 men — 100 dragoons of the regular army and 500 mounted militia. Two thousand horses and mules were needed to carry the force's supplies. To oppose this formidable array were twenty American soldiers and one civilian doctor!

LOUISIANA
◆ PURCHASE

As the tiny command started up the Missouri River on its historic adventure in July, 1806, it is perhaps well that the men did not know what they faced. Or perhaps the knowledge would only have increased Pike's determination. He was a reckless, headstrong young officer, not easily frightened.

For several hundred miles the expedition followed the yellow Missouri River westward by keelboat. About where Kansas City now stands, the stream bent north. There Pike's men traded their boats for Indian horses. On these they rode westward through what is now Kansas.

Their progress was slowed by detours to inform the Indians of the plains that the land was now claimed by the United States, not France. Another duty was to make treaties of alliance between the United States and the chiefs of the major Indian tribes. Since great ceremony attended all negotiations with the Indians, Pike was still delayed in Kansas when September arrived. He began to worry. The Rockies were an unguessable distance away, and winter was fast approaching.

Another worry came when Pike reached the main village of the Pawnees. There he learned that a large force of Spanish soldiers had been looking for him. These foreign troops had seized some American traders, though this was United States soil, and had sent the men south into Texas, which was then, of course, a Spanish possession. They had also urged the Pawnees to drive back any American soldiers who tried to march into the region. Then because the horses were worn out and the men mutinous, the Spanish commander had turned back toward Santa Fe. He was confident that the Indians, the distance, and the weather would stop the threatened invasion by the Americans.

He misjudged his man. The Spanish soldiers had no right to be in United States territory, and Pike angrily convinced the Pawnee chiefs of that fact. Having won the good will of the Indians, the Lieutenant swung southwest to the Arkansas River. There he detached six men to explore that stream to its mouth. With the remaining fifteen, Pike boldly followed the tracks of the Spanish cavalry westward into winter.

Late in November he reached the foothills of the Colorado mountains. Northward, to his right, a great rounded peak challenged his ambition. Recklessly he determined to climb it with Dr. Robinson and two soldiers.

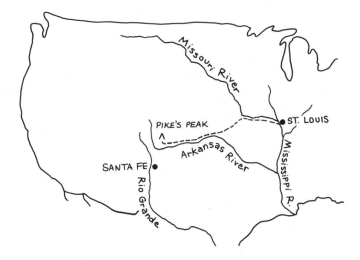

Losing their direction among the thick trees, the cliffs and the rugged gullies, the quartet emerged at dark onto the summit of a much lower spur. The snow was waist-deep. As the men huddled around their campfire, the temperature dropped below zero. Going on was clearly impossible, and in the morning Pike reluctantly turned back to his main camp. He had no way of knowing, of course, that in spite of his failure the huge summit would ever afterwards bear his name — Pikes Peak, the most famous mountain in America.

The expedition now turned into a nightmare. Possessing only summertime clothing, the reunited party floundered for a solid month through the icy gorges of the foothills. The pack horse carrying their surveying equipment fell over a cliff, and from then on they had no way of determining their position. Bewildered by the curving streams, they blundered one morning onto a camp they themselves had left weeks before.

In dismay Pike wondered what he should do next. He had three choices, all dangerous. The expedition could build shelter where it was, try to stay alive through the winter, and in the spring continue its explorations. Or the leader could, with justice, bow to the bitter winds and attempt to take his ragged men back across the plains to the settlements. Or he could make one more effort to go on — on to what?

The condition of the horses helped determine him. Exhausted by the ordeal in the foothills, the animals would need several days of rest before they could be used again. Pike was not a man to sit idle, however. Nor would he admit defeat. He decided that while the horses rested he would go ahead on foot to unravel the geography of the mountains!

It was a foolhardy decision, but his men agreed to follow him. They built a crude shelter of logs in which to store their heaviest baggage. Two men agreed to stay with the horses until the explorers either returned or sent for them. With the remaining thirteen men Pike pushed due west. Each man carried on his back weapons and equipment weighing about seventy pounds.

They fought across a tawny range of hills onto a wide plain. The temperature dropped below zero, and for four days they had nothing to eat. Two men, crippled by frozen feet, could walk no farther. Another two could progress only with the aid of canes made from tree limbs. Ahead lay a wild tumult of peaks — the Sangre de Cristo Mountains, some of their summits more than 14,000 feet high. And still Pike refused to stop.

Luckily he and Dr. Robinson succeeded in killing a buffalo. Leaving ammunition and meat with the two cripples, the able-bodied limped on, promising to send back relief as soon as possible. A howl-

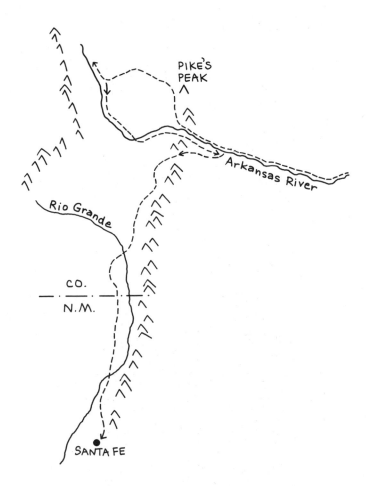

ing snowstorm delayed them, and one more man had to be abandoned with a cache of meat before the party found a pass and staggered from the mountains down into a broad, treeless valley. Beyond the valley rose the snow-shrouded peaks of the main Continental Divide.

Between the explorers and the Divide curved a south-flowing river. It was El Rio Grande del Norte — today we call it the Rio Grande — but Pike thought it might be the Red River. If so, he could float back down it to civilization. Looking for suitable timber with which to build boats, the soldiers walked wearily along the barren shore, then swung a short distance up a tributary to a pleasant grove of cottonwoods where deer abounded. Here they decided to halt.

Working with a will, they built a log fort thirty-six feet square and twelve feet high. It was additionally protected by a moat of water four feet wide and by sharpened stakes protruding over the wall. As soon as it was finished, rescuers hurried back to gather in the baggage, the horses, and the invalids.

By this time Pike and Dr. Robinson had checked their notes and had made rough calculations about where they were. Santa Fe, they decided, was no great distance away. With a recklessness that matched Pike's, Robinson now determined to venture alone through the mountains to the south and see what he could discover.

He left on February 7, 1807. Pike and his remaining "army" settled down in their fort to await whatever happened. It was not long coming. Before the absent soldiers could reappear with the horses, a hundred mounted troops appeared outside the stockade. Robinson had reached Santa Fe, and the Spanish had immediately dispatched a force back along his trail to seize the other Americans.

A parley was called. Pike was told he had trespassed on Spanish soil. He must go to Santa Fe and explain his actions to the Governor.

Thought of resistance flickered across the American's mind. A glance at his men showed that they would back him. This handful against a hundred! Protected by the fort, the Lieutenant was tempted to risk the odds. But good judgment told him that a battle inside Spanish land might cause serious trouble between the United States and Spain. Reluctantly he agreed to surrender under two conditions. First, two of his soldiers should wait at the fort with an escort of Spanish troops to help his invalids. Second, he insisted that neither he nor his men suffer the insult of being deprived of their arms.

Admiring his courage, the Spanish commander agreed. On February 27, the ragged, hungry Americans started for the forbidden capital of New Mexico. Though they kept their heads up and their muskets proudly at their sides, there was no disguising the fact that in reality they were the prisoners of an unfriendly nation.

2

Forbidden City

$\mathcal{F}$or five days and more than one hundred miles the Americans rode southward with their escort. Finally, on the afternoon of March 3, 1807, they reached a swell of low red hills that curved down from the snow-capped mountains to the east. Beyond the red hills a creek coursed westward to the Rio Grande, twelve miles or so away. Straggling along the creek was a haphazard collection of low flat-roofed houses constructed out of adobe clay.

Proudly the captain of the escort pointed. "Santa Fe!" he said, as if sure that the Americans had never in their lives seen anything resembling his native city.

He was right. They never had.

Pike, who had supposed the town to be another frontier farming village like the ones they had passed on their journey south, was amazed. This — the capital of New Mexico! To him it looked, so he wrote in his journal, like "a fleet of flat-bottomed boats."

The town was narrow and long. Its center was a large square plaza. Around the sides of this plaza, several one-story tan buildings stood shoulder to shoulder. Most were government offices, but there were also an inn, a few stores, some private residences. The doors were all low, the windows all tiny. Some of the glassless openings were protected by iron bars. A few were equipped with thin sheets of translucent mica to hold out wind and let in sunlight. Across their fronts stretched wooden awnings supported by crooked posts.

A few narrow streets opened off the plaza and wandered without plan toward the outlying homes. The buildings stood in clusters, surrounded by small fields. There the inhabitants grew grain for making their own bread and the mush they stirred into boiling water and called *atole*. Plows were mere forked sticks capped with iron. The only vehicles Pike could see were two-wheeled carts pulled by oxen. The sides of the carts were made from woven sticks, so that they looked like overgrown bird cages. Their wheels were solid round pieces of wood sawed off the end of a tree trunk. Ungreased, they emitted piercing shrieks as they rolled heavily along the rough roads.

Save for the high-spirited horse of an occasional important citizen, all other transportation seemed limited to tiny donkeys. Often only the donkeys' ears and tails and twinkling hoofs were visible beneath enormous loads of cornhusks or bundles of sticks brought down from the mountains for firewood. Plodding stolidly beside the burros were their masters, wrapped in colorful blankets and wearing tall peaked hats.

The broad, black-eyed faces of most of the humbler folk showed a strong mixture of Indian blood. Their hair was course and straight, their voices strangely soft and musical. To Pike it seemed that they must be very poor. For covering against the mountain cold the women had only shawls pulled tight about their heads and shoulders, and many of them went barefoot along the earthen paths.

Out in the plaza smoke rose lazily from cookfires where several families of Indians were camped. Everything looked raw and primitive. Pike shook his head in increased astonishment. This city was two hundred years old — far older than the scenes he was familiar with in his native New Jersey — but it certainly did not seem to have any of the settled orderliness of the eastern parts of the United States.

It was foolish to jump to conclusions, however. Santa Fe might look mean and poor to him, but at the same time he was unhappily aware that his party was creating no better impression in the eyes of the inhabitants. For months the Americans had existed with only such equipment as they could carry on their own backs. Their clothing was patched, dirty, and ragged; their whiskery faces were scorched by sun glare and wind.

Their outlandish appearance attracted a great crowd of people, who followed them through the plaza, speaking rapidly and gesturing in excitement. It was obvious that the residents of Santa Fe seldom encountered foreigners. When someone cried that these strangers were from the United States, several voices wondered aloud, in Spanish, where that could be. Pike understood enough of the language to be further mortified when he heard two woman speculating about whether the Americans lived, when at home, in houses or in tepees like Indians.

Halting on the north side of the plaza, the commander of the Spanish troops cleared a path through the crowd and led Pike into a long, low building. This, the guide said, was the Palace of the Governors.

Its magnificence, the American could not help thinking, fell short of its title. The roof consisted of layers of poles covered with sod, the floor of hard-packed earth. For rugs there were skins of bear, buffalo, and mountain lion. Strips of muslin cloth on the walls kept the whitewash from brushing off onto the clothing of persons who chanced to touch them. Mingled oddly with these humble furnishings were candlesticks of solid silver and a few pieces of massive handcarved furniture, evidently imported with great effort from distant Mexico.

When Pike was ushered into the Governor's presence, he found the man's dress and manners as rich and refined as the candlesticks. But underneath the polish was a hard suspicion. The sharp questions which the Governor asked showed that he believed the Americans were spies for an invading army and that there was nothing accidental about their having strayed onto Spanish territory.

The suspicion increased when searchers discovered in Pike's baggage certain papers that the Lieutenant had rashly tried to hide. Although the papers themselves were not of a particularly damaging nature, the attempted concealment was. In spite of Pike's continued insistence that he was an American officer surveying American territory, the Governor decided to send the party 550 painful miles farther south to Chihuahua (pronounced *Che-wa'wa*) in Old Mexico. There they would be subjected to further questioning by still higher officials.

Before the captives were marched out of Santa Fe, two Americans besought Pike's help. One, who had served as an interpreter during the talks with the Governor, was a soldier who had been captured in Texas. The other was a trapper who had wandered down alone from the Colorado mountains. The officials allowed the pair to move about Santa Fe at will, earning a living at whatever jobs they could find, but would not let them leave New Mexico. Pike, a virtual prisoner himself, could do nothing more for the men than promise to bring their case to the attention of the American government when — and if — he reached the United States.

Another foreigner in Santa Fe was the faithless trader for whom Dr. Robinson had been looking. Finding the man, however, benefited no one. The thief had squandered his profits and was living in complete poverty. Shrewdly suspecting that Robinson was trying to collect information as well as the debt, the officials had imprisoned the doctor also, in a village south of Santa Fe.

When the Americans were taken through this village on their way to Chihuahua in Old Mexico, Robinson was added to their number. Both he and Pike were keen observers; and on the harsh, month-long trip they found many thoughts to interest them.

The thing that struck Pike most forcibly was a realization of how isolated New Mexico really was. Everything a family might need — cloth, tools, hardware, dishes — had to be brought up from the south. And what a terrible trail it was! Most of the manufactured items came first by ship from the eastern United States or from England to the port of Veracruz, far south on the eastern coast of Mexico. There the objects were loaded into wagons and hauled slowly northward to Chihuahua. At Chihuahua they were transferred into carts or onto pack mules and once a year taken laboriously to Santa Fe.

All told, the land journey was 2000 miles long, much of it through blistered deserts beset by hostile Indians. As a result prices were fantastically high. For example, coarse cotton cloth of the sort that in St. Louis brought a few cents a yard, in Santa Fe cost as much as three dollars.

Thoughtfully Pike jotted the figures into a notebook he was secretly keeping. From what he had seen of the central plains on his way west, goods could be hauled easily and profitably overland straight to Santa Fe. Profits would be high, and the residents of Santa Fe would benefit from the new source of supply. But his notes about it were not a thing to let the Spanish see. They were intensely jealous of their trade privileges. If they found his papers, they would be sure that commercial as well as military spying was his reason for coming. To be on the safe side, accordingly, the Lieutenant rolled his notes into tight tubes and hid them in the barrels of his men's guns.

In Chihuahua he was again questioned closely and suspiciously. Again he insisted that he was an ordinary explorer. Unable to shake the story and fearful of complications with the United States government, the Spanish officials at last decided to turn the Americans loose.

Zebulon Montgomery Pike never returned to Mexico. (Six years later, a brigadier general, he was killed fighting the British at Toronto in the War of 1812.) But the publication of his journals brought New Mexico vividly to the attention of his countrymen.

His figures on commerce made their deepest impression in Missouri. Storekeepers in the frontier towns had a hard time disposing of goods. Money was scarce; markets were limited. But if Pike was right, out across the western horizon was a way to increase business beyond even their wildest dreams.

While the merchants were discussing the possibilities, word came that Mexico was in revolt against Spain. If the revolution succeeded, perhaps the Government's hostility toward foreigners would be ended!

Without waiting for official information, a party of trail blazers gathered together some cloth and metal goods and set hurriedly out for the once-forbidden frontiers. They were far out on the plains, beyond reach of messengers, when word seeped up the Mississippi Valley behind them that the revolt had failed. Spanish restrictions on American trade with New Mexico were certain to remain as severe as ever.

3

Trail Blazers

Ten or twelve men were in that first ill-fated party of American traders. As they came wearily out of the red hills into Santa Fe, Spanish troops seized them. In spite of their protests, they were hurried south, as Pike had been, to Chihuahua. There they were put into prison — and in prison they stayed while nine slow years dragged by.

Other adventurers had no better luck. During the years 1815-17, trappers under the command of Jules De Mun and Auguste Chouteau (pronounced *Shoo'toe*) followed Pike's trail up the Arkansas River into present-day Colorado. They caught many beaver in the mountains on the American side of the river, and were eager to extend their hunting to the Spanish side. In an effort to win permission, the two leaders, De Mun and Chouteau, rode to Santa Fe to interview the Governor.

The Governor wrote to headquarters in Mexico City, asking for instructions. When the orders came back, they were tragic. The trapping permit was not only refused, but the Americans were ordered arrested.

Two hundred dragoons of the Mexican Army clattered out of Santa Fe to the trappers' camp on the Arkansas River. Under heavy guard the captives were taken to Santa Fe and imprisoned. For forty-eight miserable days the men stayed in their cramped cells, ill fed and many of them in chains. Finally they were summoned before a panel of six judges, one of whom was the Governor. When De Mun boldly insisted that he and his men had done their trapping in American territory and that therefore they were being illegally held, the Governor flew into a rage.

Pounding the table with his fist, he shouted, so De Mun later reported, "We must have this man shot!"

Fortunately matters did not end quite so seriously. After the trial, De Mun and Chouteau were put into a single cell to await word of their fate. Presently a lieutenant unlocked the door. In his hand he carried a paper on which the sentence of the judges was written. The Americans were forced to kneel while he read it.

The order gave the trappers their liberty on the condition that they leave New Mexico immediately. But their property was confiscated — all their horses except one riding animal apiece, and $30,000 worth of furs collected through two years of labor and peril.

Such experiences completely dampened the first enthusiasm which had greeted Pike's report. Until 1821 no more efforts were made to reach New Mexico. In that year, curiously enough, three different parties started toward the west.

One was a band of trappers led by Hugh Glenn and Jacob Fowler. Their purpose was to hunt beaver on the American side of the Arkansas River. Another party moved along south of the Arkansas into what is now Oklahoma, trading with Comanche Indians. Among its members was a man named John McKnight. John's brother, Robert McKnight, had been one of the party that had hurried west after reading Pike's report and had been imprisoned in Chihuahua. It was John's hope that he could get across the border and somehow learn what had happened to the brother from whom he had received no word for nine years.

The third party consisted of five happy-go-lucky adventurers led by a veteran Indian fighter named William Becknell. These five had no definite plans. They were out following their fancy — trapping, hunting wild horses, trading with the Indians for mules and buffalo hides. For bartering they led with them a few horses loaded with things the Indians liked — brightly colored cloth, knives, kettles, looking glasses.

Becknell and his traders reached the Arkansas River in early November, a few days ahead of the trappers led by Glenn and Fowler. Instead of following the river to the front range of the Rockies as Pike had done, the wanderers left it near a side stream sometimes called the Purgatoire, sometimes the Animas, and sometimes the Picketwire. Angling southwest along the Purgatoire, they reached a gap leading through a line of high timber-covered hills running east and west. This was Raton Pass, eventually to become famous as the mountain gateway into New Mexico.

Ever since crossing the Arkansas the men had been on Spanish soil. Becknell must have known it. Nevertheless, he and his compan-

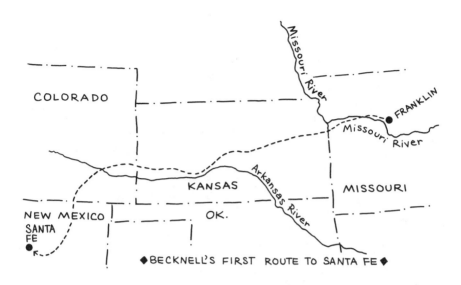

◆ BECKNELL'S FIRST ROUTE TO SANTA FE ◆

ions went gaily on into the steep hills, chopping trees and rolling boulders to clear a path for their pack animals.

Suddenly a company of dragoons appeared ahead of them. Becknell braced for trouble. Amazingly, the Americans were greeted with smiles instead of bullets. The excited talk of the soldiers soon told them why. In September Mexico had at last won her independence from Spain. Foreigners were to be welcomed now. Eagerly the troops invited Becknell's men to Santa Fe to join the celebrations and to trade if they wished.

Not long afterwards, John McKnight's party of traders left the plains and galloped into the once forbidden city. They had heard news of the revolution from *comancheros*, those wandering New Mexicans who made a risky living bartering vegetables to the Comanche Indians for dried buffalo meat. Meanwhile, Robert McKnight and his fellow prisoners had been released from the Chihuahua jail. They hurried north, and the brothers held a joyful reunion in Santa Fe. Up on the Arkansas, Hugh Glenn had also got wind of the startling developments and rode with four of his men to the Palace of the Governors to get permits for trapping the streams that had been so ruthlessly closed to De Mun and Chouteau.

Merrymaking filled Santa Fe. Except for Becknell and one other man, the Americans shared the celebration to the full. They helped cut down pine trees in the mountains, dragged them to Santa Fe, and spliced them together into a liberty pole seventy feet tall. They danced at the fandangos and cheered an independence day parade held on January 6, 1822.

They also sold the few goods they possessed at prices just as high as Lieutenant Pike had promised.

The dizzy profits had left William Becknell too impatient to wait while the celebrations in Santa Fe ran their course. Loading rawhide sacks filled with silver pesos, or Mexican dollars, onto a pack horse, he and a single reckless companion had started through the icy cold of late December to Missouri for a fresh supply of goods.

Seven weeks of hard riding brought the two men to the little frontier town of Franklin, Missouri. When the merchants in Franklin saw the sacks of silver, they went wild with excitement. Two brothers named Cooper formed a pack train and at the first hint of spring left for the new markets.

Becknell soon followed. With him were twenty-one men who had pooled their savings to buy three or four thousand dollars worth of cloth, shoes, saws, nails, glassware, and other articles which their leader knew would be in demand in New Mexico.

In order to avoid packing and repacking mules at every camp, Becknell loaded the goods into three wagons — the pioneer wagons of the western plains. The leader knew, however, that Raton Pass, through which he had ridden during his first journey, would be almost impossible for wagons. Thus it became necessary to blaze a new trail.

At a point perhaps twenty miles west of present Dodge City, Kansas, Becknell left his original route, splashed across the Arkansas River, and swung south. His intent was to reach another stream called the Cimarron. By following the Cimarron westward into New Mexico, he could avoid Raton Pass. But he did not know how terrible a desert lay ahead of him.

He soon learned. Deep sand south of the Arkansas River slowed the wagons. Under the blazing sun, men and animals suffered agonies from thirst. According to one story, the traders were about to perish when someone saw a buffalo coming from a water hole. Killing it, the men drained the water from its stomach and so were able to go on.

The trail they eventually found proved much shorter and faster than the way over Raton Pass, and during the next half century it would be the main caravan route to the Southwest. The desert between the Arkansas and Cimarron Rivers would always cause discomfort, to be sure, but the sandy wastes could be defeated if a wagon train took the simple precaution of filling its water barrels at the last crossing over the Arkansas.

♦ BECKNELL'S SECOND ROUTE TO SANTA FE ♦

A few months behind Becknell came still another group of merchants, with their goods on pack animals. This party, amazingly enough, was led by two of the men who had been jailed for nine years in Chihuahua, Samuel Chambers and James Baird. The fact that they were willing to return to New Mexico after their dreadful experience indicates the great lure which the trade held for the early pioneers.

Once again Chambers and Baird had a close brush with disaster. In southwestern Kansas a howling blizzard killed nearly every animal they owned. Unable to go on, they huddled for three months in the shelter of a cottonwood grove on an island in the Arkansas River. When spring came they hid their goods by burying them in deep pits. To secure fresh pack animals they made their way to Taos, a tiny New Mexican village of flat-roofed adobe houses some seventy miles north of Santa Fe. Returning, they unearthed their hidden merchandise and went on to eventual success. In later years the empty pits where they had buried their goods became famous landmarks, known to travelers as "The Caches."

Two years later, in 1824, William Becknell made still more history by helping to organize the trail's first full-scale merchandise caravan. In the long dusty train were twenty-two wagons, two carts, and even a small wheeled cannon for protection against the Indians. The wagons were loaded with goods worth $30,000. They returned with enormous profits — $180,000 in gold dust and silver and bundles of fur valued at another $10,000.

Such spectacular results led the United States Government to send out a party of surveyors to mark a road across the plains. After persuading the Indians to sign treaties allowing travel rights to American citizens, the surveyors plodded busily westward. Every so often they piled up large mounds of earth to show what they thought was the best route to New Mexico. The Santa Fe traders disagreed. A better way, they thought, was the trail which William Becknell, without the aid of any instruments whatsoever, had pioneered westward. The government's road was never used.

By 1826 not one but several caravans were using Becknell's trail. One of these wagon trains belonged to New Mexicans, who thereafter played an important part in the trade. In another of the 1826 caravans was sixteen-year-old Kit Carson, running away from the saddle maker to whom he was apprenticed, and bound for an eventual career as the West's most famous trapper, scout, and Indian fighter.

Many other young men joined the caravans to find excitement and fortune. It was a rollicking trip. On the plains wild lightning storms often blew down the tents. Wagons sometimes upset in the streams. An electric thrill of excitement ran through even the most experienced traders when the first shout of "Buffalo!" went up — and afterwards there were delicious feasts of fat ribs and marrow bones roasted on sticks before the campfire. Stampedes were frequent, even after the half-wild mules that pulled the wagons had traveled far enough to be trail-broken. One team would take fright, the panic would spread, and soon the whole caravan would be coursing madly across the prairie, the riders shouting in pursuit.

Many trappers accompanied the early wagon trains. These bearded beaver hunters made their headquarters in Taos, not far from an amazing terraced Indian pueblo five stories tall. From Taos the trappers spread throughout the entire Southwest, contesting nearly every foot of the way with the fierce Navajo and Apache tribes. Then back to the little village they would come with their furs, to trade in the stores that were quickly established to take care of their needs.

For most of the caravans, Santa Fe remained the goal. They came in such numbers that competition soon reduced the amount of their profits. To add to the troubles, the Mexican Government took alarm at the size of the invasion and began to impose high taxes and exasperating regulations whose main purpose seemed to be to drive the Americans out of business. Mexican traders, for example, were treated much more leniently.

In the end the difficulties strengthened the trade by leaving only able men in it. No longer could any careless adventurer slap together a load of trinkets, haul them to Santa Fe, and make himself rich. Now a man had to plan carefully, buy shrewdly, and cut to a minimum the damage suffered by his cargo as it jolted across the long trail to the mountains. In 1828 he also had to begin to worry about the Indians of the plains, who watched with deepening resentment the increased flow of white men across their lands.

4

Tribesmen & Traders Clash

Coins were scarce in New Mexico. Often the American traders had to exchange their goods for gold dust, furs, or the bright woolen blankets woven by Pueblo and Navajo Indians. Other favorite items were horses and mules, the latter of which could be resold particularly well in Missouri.

In 1828 the traders collected more than a thousand animals to take back home with them. As the party turned east along the dry bed of the Cimarron, the August heat and the dust from the huge herd grew almost unendurable. To find relief one morning when off duty, two young men named McNees and Munroe rode on ahead of the others.

Reaching a cool spring, they dismounted and drank deeply. Foolishly they then stretched out on the grass to wait for the caravan. In the drowsy heat they fell asleep. Indians saw them there, slipped up, and fell on them with tomahawks. Stealing the white men's horses and guns, the attackers vanished into the hills.

When the caravan reached the spring, McNees was dead and Munroe was dying. The sight terrified the traders. They were not trained Indian fighters. They were storekeepers, and the last thing they wanted was a battle. Fearing that Indians might still be lurking near-by, they loaded the limp bodies of their comrades into a wagon and fled forty miles farther down the Cimarron.

Along the way Munroe died. After that the traders stopped to bury the two men. By this time their panic had given way to anger and to shame at their conduct. Thus when half a dozen Comanche Indians appeared over a hill beside the new graves, no one stopped to ask if they were the ones who had killed McNees and Munroe. Probably they weren't, but rifles cracked anyhow and all but one of the Comanches dropped dead.

The lone survivor escaped into the hills and summoned his tribe. A few days later the revengeful Indians swept down on the caravan and made away with most of its thousand horses and mules. Unfortunately, that did not end the trouble. When a second caravan came along a week or so later, the Comanches attacked it also, though it, like the slain Indians, had had no part in starting the clash.

During the battle the second train lost every animal it owned. Its captain, John Means, was killed. The other men decided to try to escape on foot through the darkness; but they could not bring themselves to abandon the money they had journeyed so far to earn. Each man loaded into a pack on his back as many silver pesos as he could carry — about $1000 per man.

Covered by the night, they slipped past the Indians. For forty-eight hours they trudged northward through the desert without water or sleep. Finally they reached the Arkansas River and drank greedily of its muddy current. By this time the silver packs that once had seemed so precious had become an intolerable burden. Splashing out to an island, the men buried the treasure in the sand, even as Chambers and Baird had buried their goods after the disastrous blizzard six years earlier. They then turned east toward the settlements, more than four hundred miles away. For thirty-two starving days they walked on blistered feet under the blazing sun. Finally five of the strongest had to press on ahead and send back help for the stragglers.

These experiences led the newspapers in Missouri to demand that future caravans be protected by soldiers. The government agreed.

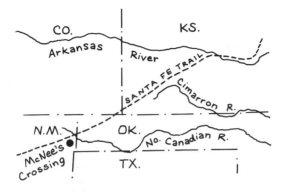

Four companies of infantry were ordered to escort the spring caravan of 1829 to the Mexican border along the Arkansas River, which was as far as American troops could legally go.

To the unhappy traders this was not far enough. The Comanche attacks had taken place south of the Arkansas on Mexican ground. Renewed hostilities would probably occur in the same area. If so, the caravan would lack protection just when soldiers were most needed. Indeed, the prospect was so discouraging that when spring drew near, all but eleven men backed down. These were not enough to justify a caravan, and it began to look as if the Santa Fe trade might come to an inglorious end.

At this point there appeared on the scene the brothers Charles and William Bent. Short, stocky and black-haired, they were trained in the ways of the wilderness. William Bent, though only twenty that spring, had been trading for at least four years among the Indians of the upper Missouri and Platte Rivers. His brother Charles, nine years older, had already made a striking reputation for himself as a trapper operating as far away as the Rocky Mountains in present-day Wyoming and Utah.

Recently a series of disasters had bankrupted Charles Bent's trapping company. In an effort to regain his fortune, he had borrowed money from friends and relatives and had bought goods to sell in Santa Fe. Now he found the merchants were talking of not sending a caravan to New Mexico this year!

No mere Indian scare was enough to stop either Bent. When Charles let it be known that he and William, together with the veteran

Waldo brothers, were going to push ahead regardless of the Comanches, several other merchants took heart. All told, 79 men agreed to drive a total of 38 wagons across the long trail. This was a poor showing, however, when compared to the 200 men and 100 wagons of the previous year. In spite of the Bents and the troops, most of the frontier merchants still preferred to stay safely at home.

Until 1828 the starting point of the Santa Fe trade had been the town of Franklin on the north bank of the Missouri River. But in that year a flood had washed most of the village into the river. Accordingly the Bents, whose home was St. Louis, chose another embarkation point. On a steamer they churned with their goods up the yellow river to the very border of Kansas. There, two miles back from the south bank of the stream, stood the little log town of Independence.

Here Major Bennet Riley was supposed to meet the caravan with his troops. While the traders waited, they looked around and liked what they saw. Because the river bent north at this point, Independence was as close to New Mexico as steamboats could get. All around were grassy fields where great numbers of livestock could be pastured. The combination was ideal. From this time on, Independence would achieve growing fame as the jumping-off point both for the Southwest and for Oregon.

When at last Major Riley's soldiers came into sight, the traders grew furious. The troopers were on foot! Even worse, the military baggage had been loaded into wagons pulled by lumbering oxen. How could such an escort possibly keep up with the caravan, most of whose men rode horseback and whose wagons were pulled by fast-stepping mules?

Since trouble was not expected for many miles, Riley started his infantry down the trail ahead of the caravan. Behind him, the traders elected Charles Bent captain of their train, and in noisy confusion set out across the greening prairie to overtake the escort. Amazingly, they had trouble doing it. The soldiers, far better disciplined than the traders, were able to make and break camp each day much more quickly than the civilians. Their oxen were easier to handle and could pull heavier loads than the half-wild mules of the merchants. Thoughtfully, Charles Bent admitted that his first opinion at Independence had been wrong. The traders, not the military escort, were the slow part of the caravan.

Without incident the travelers reached the point on the Arkansas River where they had to leave Riley's escort and cross unprotected into Mexican territory. Losing heart, some of the men tried to persuade the Major to continue. He refused, as he was bound to do under international law. During the argument, men who had survived the Indian attacks of the previous autumn rode to the island where they had buried their silver. When they returned, the sight of so many gleaming pesos helped inspire the more timid of the merchants to press ahead.

Whooping and shouting, they spent a full day forcing their wagons through the quicksand of the river. The next dawn they started single file through low, barren hills. In the sandy soil the weaker teams fell behind. Even the stronger ones had difficulty. By afternoon they had traveled fewer than nine miles.

The awkward, straggling progress worried Charles Bent. He kept trying to pull the train into a more compact knot. Before he could manage, he heard the war shriek he had been dreading. Looking up, he saw three of the advance guard racing wildly back toward the lead wagons. Behind them dashed a horde of Indians. Even as Charles sized up the situation, the Indians overtook the slowest of the trio and struck him down.

Panic turned most of the merchants helpless, but Charles put spurs to his horse, let out a ferocious howl and charged straight toward the attackers! His brother William swept up beside him. Both were expert riders and marksmen. Their wild, banging rush dismayed the foremost Indians and drew attention from the caravan. The startled warriors swung aside, and the two brothers stopped between them and the caravan, holding their nervous horses back to back. From that position they could see and check every hostile motion, for their cocked rifles had a longer range than the bows and poor muskets of the Indians.

During the pause the merchants got hold of themselves, grouped the wagons in a defensive circle, and began digging rifle pits. Covered by their guns, the Bent brothers dropped back to shelter. Nine volunteers, inspired by their bravery, now started for Major Riley's camp on the Arkansas for help. The same sort of fierce bluff that had saved the wagon train enabled them to break through the line of Indians. Forgetting the fine points of international law, Riley ordered his soldiers across the river. Hearing the bugles, the Indians melted away into the hills.

Trouble was not ended, however. Unwilling to risk complications by staying on Mexican soil, Riley returned with his soldiers to the north bank of the Arkansas, where he planned to wait until the caravan returned in the fall. The troops had scarcely vanished when a crowd of Mexican buffalo hunters reached the caravan with word that Indians from miles around were joining the war parties. In terror the newcomers begged permission to accompany the American merchants to Santa Fe.

Charles agreed, and the motley group crept up the Cimarron toward the mountains. Indians hung on their flanks, just out of range, hoping to pick off stragglers. To Charles Bent, however, the worst enemies were lack of sleep and the unthinking fear of most of his men. He had to be everywhere at once, setting out guards, giving encouragement, making plans.

Just as he was reaching the end of his endurance, a band of trappers galloped down from the Taos mountains. A messenger had reached them with word that their countrymen were being besieged, and every American in northern New Mexico joined forces to ride to the rescue.

At this gathering there was a dramatic meeting between the Bent brothers and two men who would be their lifelong friends. One was Kit Carson, almost the same age as young William Bent. The other was a great laughing, black-bearded Frenchman named Céran St. Vrain.

Discouraged by the appearance of the trappers, the Indians switched their attention to Riley's camp on the Arkansas. Throughout the summer they made hit-and-run attacks on it, killing two or three men and seizing several horses.

Meanwhile the merchants were succeeding well with their trading. Although William Bent stayed in the mountains to trap, Charles was so encouraged by his adventure that he determined to go back with Céran St. Vrain to Missouri for another supply of goods. An escort of Mexican soldiers accompanied the returning caravan. One sharp battle with the Indians on the Cimarron ended difficulties from that quarter. The wayfarers rejoined Riley on the Arkansas, and the rest of the journey home passed without event.

5

Caravans Roll

*O*ne result of the desperate but successful trip of 1829 was the formation of the best-known trading firm in the Southwest: Bent, St. Vrain & Company. Another result was the establishment of methods of travel which would last, with little change, for the next half century. In both developments, energetic Charles Bent played the leading part.

The Santa Fe trade was based largely on speculation. A proprietor, as the owner of goods was called, bought his supplies in Missouri on credit. This meant that he had to sell his merchandise in New Mexico as fast as possible and then hurry back to the United States to settle his debts. Since the goods reached the Santa Fe markets at the same time, prices dropped when the caravans arrived. If a man could somehow wait there a few months, he was almost certain to find business better.

Why not solve the difficulty, Charles Bent wondered, by forming a partnership? One partner could stay in New Mexico to sell the goods when prices rose, and the other could freight in fresh supplies. If the freighting partner moved fast enough across the hundreds of miles of prairie, he might even be able to take two trips a year and so reach the market during the off seasons with whatever goods were most in demand.

Two trips in one summer? The other traders laughed the scheme off as completely wild. But not Céran St. Vrain. His imagination was as keen as Charles Bent's.

Céran was the son of a French nobleman who had been driven from his native land to America by the French Revolution. For a time the younger St. Vrain had traded along the Missouri with other Frenchmen from St. Louis. Then in 1825 he had gone to Taos. Since that time he had trapped beaver and had fought Indians throughout New Mexico and Arizona. As already noted, he had met Charles Bent when he had ridden with a band of mountain men down from Taos to rescue the 1829 caravan. From that meeting came a friendship that eventually grew into the partnership Charles had dreamed of.

Céran St. Vrain spoke Spanish well. He knew Mexican customs and had many friends. It would be a joy, he said, not to have to leave his home in New Mexico half of every year just for supplies. He would be happy to run the stores in Santa Fe and Taos — the men planned establishments in both towns — while Charles took care of business in the East and brought in the goods.

Thus the firm of Bent, St. Vrain & Company was founded. Straightway Charles turned back to Independence. In 1830 he not only made the "impossible" two trips across the plains, but journeyed south into Old Mexico as well. The next year he made two more crossings. On the second trip he brought still another change to the trail — a caravan pulled entirely by oxen.

Until that time the traders had used mules. They thought oxen could not make the long trip west. Mules were faster and had tougher hoofs. But mules were expensive. They were also a great temptation to Indians, who were always likely to raid a caravan in an effort to steal the long-eared animals. But no Indian wanted an ox. The ungainly creatures could not be ridden, and to an Indian ox meat did not taste nearly as good as buffalo steak.

Reflecting on these things and remembering how well oxen had pulled Major Riley's baggage wagons in 1829, Charles Bent determined to experiment with cattle. He had picked a dangerous time. September of 1831 was at hand when he began loading his wagons in Independence. If oxen were as slow as the pessimists in the town warned him, snowstorms might catch the caravan before it reached the Rockies.

Charles did not listen. By now he knew the plains as well as any man — how to load, how to travel, how to camp — and he was sure he could get the oxen through. Carefully he inspected each wagon to make certain its axles and tongue were sound and strong. He lined the sides of the bed with canvas to keep out rain. Boxes and bales were carefully stowed so that no shift in weight would unbalance the vehicle in a ticklish spot.

Over the top of the bed were arched high wooden bows. Double sheets of canvas were stretched over these bows. As further protection against the weather, Mackinaw blankets were spread between the sheets of canvas.

At least eight mules or the same number of oxen were needed to pull the huge wagons, some of which carried two and a half tons of cargo and had wheels as high as a man's head. Most of the draft animals that the traders bought in Independence had never worn a harness, let alone pulled such a wagon as those. No matter. The half-wild beasts were driven into corrals, roped amidst choking clouds of dust, and forcibly hitched into teams. Mules brayed, oxen bawled, tug chains rattled. Stampeding teams galloped in all directions before the shouting men finally brought them under control.

The majority of the proprietors owned only one or two wagons and made only a single trip a year, leaving as soon as the grass was up in the spring. Since little danger was encountered on the first section of the trail, the wagons pulled out of Independence one by one, as fast as they were made ready. A shakedown journey of one hundred and fifty miles brought them to Council Grove, a lovely stretch of forest land in the broad valley of the Neosho River.

Council Grove boasted excellent grass and water. It also furnished the last stand of good hardwood trees the caravans would pass. Accordingly the region became a favorite gathering place for the Santa Fe caravans. Here last-minute repairs were made. Here spare axles and wagon tongues were cut. Most importantly, here the train was given its organization.

Some form of discipline was essential. Each spring a hundred or more wagons manned by several hundred lively young roustabouts and pulled by a thousand head of livestock gathered for the trip. To make plans and give orders, captains and lieutenants were elected by democratic vote. These captains then assigned each wagon its place in the train. They divided the men into watches for standing guard during lonely nights. Along the way they decided, according to conditions, the length of each day's march and the location of each night's camp.

Only officers with sound judgment and strong leadership were able to keep the ponderous train moving in unison, with a minimum of quarrels. Because the proprietors were headstrong men and wanted their own way, no captain and no plan ever suited everyone. Yet by and large, the American form of self-government which the merchants worked out succeeded. Without it the unwieldy caravans could hardly have operated as well as they did.

All this was familiar to Charles Bent. He had been captain of the 1829 caravan and would be elected again in 1832 and 1833. But in the fall of 1831 the situation was different. First, there were the oxen. Second, there was no need of an election, for all ten wagons in the small train belonged to Bent, St. Vrain & Company. And finally, each of the thirty or forty men had been hired by Charles and was directly responsible to him.

They were young men, as were the workers in all the caravans. Some had grown up on farms along the frontier. Some were native New Mexicans wearing peaked hats, bright serapes, and leather trousers. There were singing French Canadians in gaudy calico shirts. There were tall Delaware Indians, hired as hunters to supply the caravan with meat. And in nearly every caravan there was at least one tenderfoot from the East, hunting adventure before settling down to some routine business. Accompanying Charles Bent in 1831, for example, was Albert Pike (no relation to Zebulon Pike), twenty-one years old, his six-foot frame restless with energy. Later Pike would become a poet, a newspaperman, a Confederate general, and the author of one of the many versions of the South's favorite song, "Dixie."

Following the example of the spring caravans, Charles paused at Council Grove to make sure that everything was shipshape. The morning of departure dawned on electric expectancy. Even before the sun had cleared the low hills, Charles was shouting the familiar "Catch up! Catch up!"

Eager to be the first to hitch their teams, each wagon crew rushed from the breakfast fires into the temporary corrals. To save trouble in harnessing, the oxen had been left yoked in pairs when turned loose before dawn to graze. Even so, some were difficult to handle. There were scuffles and oaths and a crackle of whips before a triumphant voice sang out the first "All set!"

Other voices followed. When every wagon was ready, Charles shouted, "Stretch out!" With a rumble of wheels, the line pointed toward the west.

The wagons traveled in double rows so that in case of alarm they could swing quickly into a defensive square. (Where ground allowed, larger caravans traveled in four lines.) As they neared stream crossings, workers went ahead with shovels to smooth down the banks and bridge boggy places with mats of willow brush and long grass.

In the evenings the wagons were parked in a square, their tongues pointing outside. During the early years of the trade the draft animals were allowed to graze at dusk and in the morning, and at night were penned inside the ring of wagons. Later it was learned that both mules and oxen could be picketed by long ropes fastened to pegs driven into grassy spots just outside the corral. This method saved the work of herding and allowed the animals more time for eating. From that point on, the animals were driven inside the corral only in case of alarm and for catching in the morning.

In order to keep the corral clear for the morning catching, cookfires were built outside the square. The men slept outside also, on buffalo robes, the stars their only roof except when thunderstorms sent them crawling under the wagons for shelter.

The average day's travel was from fifteen to twenty miles. Oxen, Charles noted with satisfaction, made the distance as easily as mules did. True, some of the cattle developed sore feet, but he remedied the difficulty by making shoes for them out of leather. The device worked well in dry weather, but wet grass soon rotted the moccasins.

Two hundred and seventy miles from Independence the caravan reached the yellow sandhills bordering the Arkansas River. The sprawling, shallow stream was dotted by islands green with cottonwood trees. For a hundred and twenty miles the traders followed its valley westward. They carved their names in the soft red sandstone of Pawnee Rock. They swatted mosquitoes and saw strange mirages of hill-bordered lakes hanging upside down in the sky.

Animal life was everywhere. Packs of wolves followed the huge herds of buffalo. Antelope and jackrabbits bounded by with unbelievable speed. In places rattlesnakes were so thick that the drovers went ahead of the train with guns to keep the animals from being bitten.

Presently the time came to ford the Arkansas and strike south to the Cimarron. Charles knew that the river bottom was dangerous with quicksand. To keep the wagons from settling they were hurried across behind doubled teams. In the excitement mules were likely to plunge, fall down, and even drown before they could be cut loose from the harness. But the oxen, Charles was happy to see, pulled steadily, without panic.

The crossing completed, the men filled water barrels for the dry *jornada* (or journey) to the Cimarron. From eastbound travelers they learned that the dread stretch once again had taken its toll. Early in the spring a train belonging to Jedediah Smith and William Sublette had become confused by crisscrossing buffalo trails and had missed the way. As thirst began to torment the men, Jedediah Smith rode off alone to look for water. He was perhaps the West's greatest pioneer. He had found new trails into California and Oregon. He had survived one massacre after another. But in the Cimarron desert, Comanches caught him off guard and struck him down.

Warned by the tragedy, Charles Bent's caravan had no trouble either with thirst or Indians. Their misery came from the weather. A blue-white lightning bolt on the Cimarron stampeded their livestock. A wild chase recovered most of the animals, but not the saddle horse belonging to young Albert Pike. He had to walk the rest of the way to New Mexico.

After following the Cimarron about eighty miles, the trail swung southwest to the headwaters of the Canadian River. The mountains were in sight now. Frost had stripped the leaves from the aspen trees and the November nights were cold. But Charles could not hurry. The dry air had shrunk the wood of the wagons. A halt had to be made. To the tune of clanging hammers, the loose spokes and iron tires were wedged tight again.

At the Canadian River the trail forked. The principal branch paralleled the mountains for several miles, then looped west through a pass and came into Santa Fe from the south. It was an exciting goal. The men slicked up their long hair, put on clean shirts saved just for this, and wove new poppers into their whips. As the wagons trundled down into the dusty streets, the whole town ran out to welcome them.

On this trip, however, Charles was bound not for Santa Fe, but for Bent, St. Vrain & Company's new store in Taos, the little village

seventy miles north of the capital city. His way led directly west across the Sangre de Cristo Mountains. Before he reached the summit, a blizzard howled down on the caravan. Gasping in the sleet, the men cut evergreen boughs and heaped them around the wagon wheels, building cave-like shelters. There they huddled for a week of bitter cold. One horse and six or eight oxen froze to death before enough snow melted so that they could creep on to their destination.

It had been a close call. But traders everywhere realized if oxen could get through that late in the year, they could certainly do it in the spring. More and more proprietors switched to cattle, and the humble ox became one of the chief factors in the opening of the West.

6

Biggest Trading Post in the West

*Y*oung William Bent was the one who first thought of building a trading post on the Arkansas River. He wanted a safe place in which to barter with the tribes of the high plains. He felt he could make the establishment succeed, for he knew Indians well, both from teen-age experiences along the Missouri River and from what he had picked up in the Southwest after arriving at Santa Fe with his brother Charles in 1829.

William's first adventure had been a trapping trip to the Gila River (pronounced *Hee'la*) in what is now Arizona. On the Gila more than a hundred warriors armed with bows and arrows had attacked his small party. Although the whites were better armed than the Indians, they had been lucky to escape with their lives. After the experience some of the men gave up the wilderness. But not William. He secured fresh supplies and new campanions in Taos and went into the mountains of southern Colorado. The adventurers caught few beaver there, for the streams had been overtrapped, but they had good luck trading with the Cheyenne and Arapaho tribesmen roaming along the eastern base of the Rockies.

Encouraged by this, William built a crude stockade of cottonwood logs on the Arkansas River not far east of the deep gorge through which the stream breaks out of the mountains. The tall, lithe Cheyennes, perhaps the best horsemen of the plains, flocked into his station, bringing him shaggy buffalo robes in exchange for cooking pots, hunting knives, beads, vermilion, powder, and lead. William learned their language, shared their wild-riding sports. He further won their esteem when he hid two of them in his camp and then bluffed off an arrogant war party of Comanches who were out looking for the Cheyennes' scalps.

His trade grew to such an extent that he had difficulty finding enough supplies in Santa Fe. So in 1832 when Charles arrived in New Mexico as captain of the big spring caravan, William met him with a startling plan. Why not shift some of these goods from Santa Fe to the Arkansas?

The older brother hesitated. He and Céran St. Vrain were establishing a reputation as the leading merchants of New Mexico. Their business in Taos and Santa Fe was safe. The Indian trade was always dangerous. Why not let things stay the way they were?

William, however, was persuasive. And the Bents had always thrived on risk. With a sudden smile, Charles nodded. He would take the chance!

Two more Bent brothers had come west with Charles that spring. They were George, aged eighteen, and Robert, aged sixteen. To the boys the new plan was an exciting experience, for it involved taking several wagons loaded with supplies into country where wagons never before had gone. It also involved, they soon discovered, a great deal of hard work.

From Santa Fe they went back along the regular trail to the point where it left the Canadian River. Here William guided the wagons due north. Ahead of the hard-used vehicles, stretching eastward from the front range of the Rockies, was a jumble of square-topped hills. Opening through this barrier of forest and canyon was a gap known to horsemen as Raton Pass.

Eleven years before, William Becknell had had so much trouble getting his horses through Raton that thereafter he had avoided the pass and instead had brought his wagons up the Cimarron. Wheels, it was thought, could not go any other way. But the Bents were a stubborn family, not used to turning back. Foot by foot they chopped out a passage through the pine trees. They pried boulders loose with long wooden poles and shoveled down sidehills level enough for the creaking wheels.

Wearily they came down the north side of the Raton Mountains and reached at last the lovely meadows where Trinidad, Colorado, now stands. Winding through these meadows was the creek variously called the Purgatoire, Purgatory, Picketwire, or the Animas — shortened forms of the full-resounding Spanish name of El Rio de las Animas Perdidas en Purgatorio: The River of Lost Souls in Purgatory.

Beyond the meadows the Purgatoire plunged into a grim brown canyon too rough even for the Bent brothers. Leaving the stream, they rattled off among black piñon trees onto an alkali plain studded with cactus. Presently they reached another creek, dry in summer, called Timpas. This they followed toward its junction with the winding Arkansas.

Cheyenne Indian friends of William's met them and persuaded them to turn down the Arkansas instead of up it toward the stockade William had been using near the mountains. Soon the train reached a broad bench, good for camping. (On a modern map the site lies between the Colorado cities of La Junta and Las Animas.) It caught the brothers' eyes. There was enough grass in the valley bottom for hundreds of head of livestock, enough cottonwood trees for fuel and for building material. More importantly, so the Cheyennes said, good trails led from the bench deep into the heart of the buffalo range. And as Charles knew, the price paid in St. Louis for buffalo robes was steadily rising.

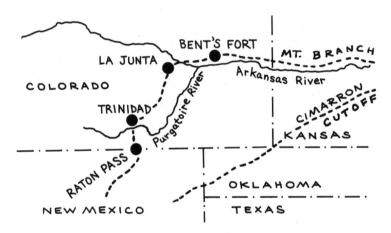

As the oldest Bent studied the land, he reached a bold decision. If they were going to enter the Indian trade, why not do it with every resource they could command? Rather than start with another small log stockade such as William had used, they would build the largest trading post the American West had yet known!

Back in Taos, they consulted with Céran St. Vrain. He agreed to help finance the project, and plans were quickly formed. The Bents, it was decided, would take to Missouri the money and livestock the firm had accumulated during two years of trading — $190,000 in gold dust, silver, furs, and mules. Charles would stay in Missouri during the winter to make ready the next year's supply train, but William would return ahead of him with tools and hardware to be used in the fort. Céran meanwhile would assemble a hundred or so Mexican workers, take them to the Arkansas, and start the construction.

During the summer of 1833 the great walls slowly took shape. The area they embraced was considerably larger than a modern football field. The back, or western, section was designed as a corral big enough to hold, in a pinch, 400 head of horses. Its walls were eight feet high. Cactus was planted on their broad tops to keep Indians from trying to scale them. In the spring the prickly plants furnished, in addition to protection, spectacular displays of red and white blossoms.

The business part of the fort lay in the eastern section. Here the walls were fourteen feet high. Squat towers rose at the southeast and northwest corners and protruded in such a way that defenders shooting through loopholes could sweep all four walls with rifle fire.

The main gate, sheathed with iron, faced east toward approaching caravans. Above the gate was a watch tower equipped with a telescope. Above the tower was a bell for summoning the workers to their meals. Two trained eagles for several years used the belfry as a roost. Above their home, fittingly enough, rose a flagstaff bearing the Stars and Stripes.

Against the four walls of the eastern square and surrounding a central court called the *placita* was built a series of rooms — warehouses, kitchen, mess hall, shops, and living quarters for the workers and their Indian families. When operations reached full swing, more than a hundred persons inhabited the fort and it became necessary to build a second tier of rooms on top of the northern section. On the second story too, was the large apartment of the owners.

Except for roof timbers and support posts, the entire structure was built Mexican fashion from adobe bricks. Water and clay were mixed to a stiff mud in several shallow pits. Coarse wool and grass were added as binding material. The mud was then packed into wooden molds and dried into bricks eighteen inches long, twelve wide, four thick. Tens of thousands of these heavy bricks had to be patiently made and patiently carried up ladders to tops of the rising walls.

There was never any doubt as to who should be manager of the huge establishment. Céran St. Vrain could not be. He was needed in New Mexico to handle the trade there. Charles was often away with the caravans. George and Robert were inexperienced. Thus the responsibility fell on the man who first proposed the idea — William Bent, not yet twenty-five years old when operations began late in the fall of 1833.

The company named the place for him — Fort William. But the trappers who came down from the mountains to spend their winters there, to buy supplies and sell beaver pelts, never called it that. To them it was Bent's Fort, and by that name it became the most famous landmark in the Southwest.

Sometimes hundreds of tall conical Indian tepees dotted the ground outside its walls. Travelers and adventurers made it their goal. Army expeditions used it as a base of supplies. Keeping its force of workers supplied with buffalo meat required the services of several expert hunters. For years one of them was Kit Carson.

Bent, St. Vrain caravans broke out a new road up the Arkansas to the fort and improved the way which the brothers had blazed through Raton Pass. Soon this route past the fort into New Mexico became known as the mountain branch of the Santa Fe Trail.

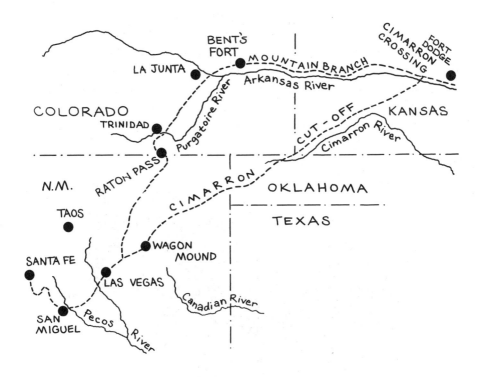

The mountain branch had several advantages over the old route along the Cimarron. Wood and water were more abundant, and the fort made a welcome resting place. But the Raton way was longer than the Cimarron way. To wagon trains creaking ahead at fifteen or twenty miles a day the extra distance was a thing to be avoided. Accordingly the bulk of the travel continued its dusty way along the Cimarron. But whenever a caravan needed repairs or feared for its safety, it could always find help at Bent's Fort.

With the powerful Cheyenne and Arapaho Indians, the Bents and their partners formed a lasting peace. The other tribes, however, were less friendly. In 1837 Pawnees captured an entire Bent, St. Vrain

& Company mule train in Raton Pass. The next year Comanches raided the horse herd at the gates of the fort itself, killing two men before being driven off. And in 1841 a war party killed the youngest of the Bent brothers, Robert, out hunting buffalo and took his scalp.

In spite of these things American power in the Southwest continued to grow. The Bents and St. Vrain built additional forts to the north and to the south. Increasing numbers of merchants found their way down both branches of the trail to the once-forbidden city of Santa Fe. From there American goods spread farther and farther through the land — deep into Old Mexico and westward to the Pacific.

7

Beyond Santa Fe

*T*oday, competition between storekeepers does not sound exciting. But in New Mexico in the 1830's a man often had to be a combination scout, wagon master, horseman, and Indian fighter to stay ahead of his rivals.

As the competition in Santa Fe increased, many merchants, including several Mexicans, followed the lead of Bent, St. Vrain & Company in keeping their stores open throughout the year. But soon this was not enough. The poor people of New Mexico could not absorb all the barrels of nails, bolts of cloth, and boxes of spice that came pouring in from the United States, and it was then necessary for the merchants to seek new markets.

Only two districts existed where buyers lived. One was the northern part of Old Mexico, where trade centered around the ancient silver-mining city of Chihuahua. The other was the cluster of hamlets growing up around the missions in California.

American traders confined themselves almost entirely to northern Mexico. The distances from Santa Fe were comparatively short, and a known trail, centuries old, wound south along the Rio Grande. Even so, it was not an easy way.

First, an exasperating amount of paper work had to be attended to. The law required a list in Spanish of every article carried in the wagons. Complicated passports and trading permits had to be secured. Fees were high and New Mexican officials moved slowly. Often they had to be bribed to do their jobs.

If some other official farther down the line detected the least mistake in the forms, he was entitled to confiscate the entire cargo. As a result when the merchants approached the customs houses in Old Mexico, they held their breath in an agony of suspense, wondering whether they would be allowed to pass without losing everything they owned.

The Apaches were an even greater threat. Their fierce raids caused the abandonment for several years of mail service between Santa Fe and Chihuahua. Because of their continual attacks, settlers forsook entire towns, like Valverde, a hundred miles below Albuquerque. At times the Apaches swooped boldly into the very outskirts of El Paso and even of Chihuahua itself, attacking villagers at work in their gardens.

The Comanches added to the danger. Each year they moved south from Texas to replenish their horse herds by raiding the ranches of Old Mexico. Often they seized captives, particularly children. Some of these prisoners were ransomed from the Indians years later by the Bents as far away as the fort on the Arkansas. Other Mexicans grew to like their captors, stayed with them and became important members of the tribe, even leading raids against their former homelands. Still other raiders had no connection with the Indians at all, but were bandits disguised to look like Apaches or Comanches.

Because of these threats, the American merchants dared not travel south except in strong, heavily armed caravans. Because of their strength they were seldom attacked, and Mexican mule drivers often joined forces with them.

The worst stretch of their road was in southern New Mexico, where a range of barren mountains forced the muddy Rio Grande through a deep canyon. Here the wagons had to leave the river and

go east down the other side of the mountains. This stricken piece of wasteland, ninety miles long, the Mexicans called by a name which they gave to nearly every sun-blasted stretch of desert in the Southwest — Jornada del Muerto, Dead Man's Journey.

Men could carry water for themselves across the Jornada. Animals, however, often suffered cruelly, even when traveling was done in the cool of night. Only a single spring existed along the way, and it lay five or six miles off to the side in a deep gorge so gloomy and so suited to ambush that travelers seldom sought its water except in emergency.

Sixty miles below the Jornada the caravans came to a ford over the Rio Grande. If the river was high, the goods had to be ferried to the southern shore in dugout canoes, and the wagons were then floated across empty. At low water the wagons could be dragged across — provided they did not stick in the quicksand. Either method was so troublesome that travelers approaching the ford hardly knew whether to wish for deep water or shallow.

Beyond the ford sprawled the old city of El Paso. (Today the town is called Cuidad Juárez [pronounced *Seyoo dad' Hwa'rez*]; the American city of El Paso on the north bank of the river is comparatively new.) In the 1830's, Mexican El Paso was not so much a city as a long stretch of fertile farmland in which were dotted clusters of houses and barns. In the largest of these clusters was the customs house with its dreaded inspectors.

By this time the caravans had journeyed 320 miles from Santa Fe and some of them were content to stop. Most, however, pushed on 230 more miles to Chihuahua. The worst stretch on this lower trail was Los Médanos, exhausting sandhills thirty miles south of El Paso. Teams could not pull loaded wagons through the deep, soft sand. The goods had to be carried over on specially hired pack mules and then laboriously reloaded. After that, the journey settled down to endless hours of glaring sun, low hills, and drab forests of mesquite.

The average journey to Chihuahua took forty days. If a trader was lucky, he might sell his goods wholesale to a local merchant and be free to return home within a week. Otherwise he had to sell the merchandise retail, item by item, spending long evenings in his rented store building while the women of Chihuahua wandered slowly by, fingering his offerings by candlelight. Sometimes even this effort failed. Then the unfortunate merchant had to go through the ordeal of securing new permits, reloading his wagons, and rattling on south to the trading fairs that were held from time to time in little towns in the remote mountains.

Their business finished, some of the merchants made their way to the coast and caught ships back to the United States. Most, however, returned to Santa Fe. Since they generally had sold their wagons in Chihuahua, they had to travel by horseback. Transporting the coins they had gathered was difficult, for a loose mass of copper and silver money was hard to handle on mule back. To overcome this, the traders often wrapped the coins in rawhide sacks. The leather was then soaked in water. As it dried, it shrank, compressing the loose money into a bundle as solid and heavy and easy to pack as a chunk of concrete.

Aside from northern Mexico, the only other markets for American goods were San Diego and the missions near what is now Los Angeles. The way was long and hard, broken by lofty mountains, vast red canyons, and deserts far worse than the Jornada del Muerto. Indeed, the obstacles were so great that the Spanish had never succeeded in opening a trail between Santa Fe and the coast. That accomplishment waited for American trappers seeking restlessly for new sources of beaver fur.

At first the trappers went west along the Gila River of Arizona, but Apaches in that section were so fierce and the deserts of the interior part of southern California so blazing hot that later parties worked out safer routes to the north. In time this northern way came to be known as the Old Spanish Trail, although the western part of it was actually the youngest of the historic trails of the Southwest.

It was called old because the first section of it followed tracks left by a Spanish explorer named Escalante. In 1776, the year of the American Declaration of Independence, Escalante had tried to find a way from Santa Fe to Monterey in central California. From New Mexico the explorer had gone across the southwestern corner of what is now Colorado into Utah. There he had turned back. But half a century later, in 1831, American trappers under William Wolfskill had found a way to go on and still avoid the tremendous red gorges that run into the Grand Canyon of the Colorado. They did it by skirting the high mountains west of present Zion National Park, then threading the lower reaches of Nevada and pushing thirstily on across the Mojave Desert to the green valleys of the coast.

Weather was as grim an opponent as the harsh land. In the gasping heat of summer a crossing of the California deserts was almost impossible. Travelers therefore chose to go in the spring. But this meant the risk of encountering snow in the mountains of Colorado and Utah. Wolfskill's trappers survived one blizzard only by building a crude windbreak of brush, blankets, and priceless beaver pelts. In this costly shelter, with wood enough available for only one small fire, the men and their livestock huddled close together for several days of icy misery.

Such a route could not be used by wagons. That may be one reason why the Americans, though they found the trail, let the trade with California fall into the hands of Mexican mule drivers called *arrieros* (pronounced *ah ree ehr' os*).

Cloth and blankets were the principal articles of commerce. Bulky packs weighing two or three hundred pounds each were lashed on to the backs of mules so wild that they had to be blindfolded during the loading. One of the mules in the train always carried a grindstone, on which the drovers ground the grain for their simple meals. Mush from this pulverized grain, a few beans, some fiery *chili* and occasional feasts of deer meat were the only food the men had during a trip that lasted nearly three months each way.

In California the cloth and blankets were exchanged for horses and mules. These herds were driven back to Santa Fe and traded to

Americans who took them to Missouri. In that state the long-eared part of the herds became famous, wrongly enough, as "Missouri mules." They should have been called California mules.

Not all the mules were obtained by honest trade. California was so full of livestock that many of the animals were let run half wild. Word of this reached shadowy gangs of bandits call *chaguanosos* (pronounced *chah wahn oh' sos*). Renegade Indians and a few of the wilder trappers joined these outlaw gangs, and for several years their sudden, springtime raids spread terror through the California *ranchos*. In April, 1840, more than a thousand head were stolen away from the mission of San Luis Obispo alone.

Surprisingly enough, this mule and horse stealing by the *chaguanosos* was almost the only outlawry connected with the far-flung Santa Fe trade. Even caravans returning to Missouri loaded with gold and precious furs were seldom molested. One reason for the lawfulness was the rugged nature of the caravan guards. No one wanted to pick a fight with them. Another reason was the prompt action of the United States Army when one group of raiders from Texas did move north, in hope of causing trouble.

8

Raiders from Texas

*I*n 1836, in an upheaval destined to spread confusion and trouble all along the trail from Missouri to Santa Fe, the huge province of Texas revolted against Mexico. After several setbacks the rebel army, led by Sam Houston, finally defeated the Mexicans at San Jacinto (pronounced *San Hasin'to*). The jubilant victors thereupon proclaimed Texas an independent republic.

Feeling its oats, the new nation next claimed, among other things, boundaries reaching as far westward as the Rio Grande. This meant, in the eyes of the rebels at least, that Santa Fe, Taos, and most of the other towns in New Mexico were now a part of the Republic of Texas.

The government of Mexico refused to recognize the claim — or, indeed, any other statement by the Texans. Officials in Santa Fe likewise ignored them. The attitude in New Mexico seemed to be, Why worry? Did not several hundred miles of hostile wilderness lie between Texas and the Rio Grande?

For years nothing was done. The government of the new Republic of Texas was too poor and was having too much trouble establishing order at home to waste energy reaching out into New Mexico. In 1841, however, a group of private citizens, mostly Americans who had emigrated to Texas, decided to take matters into their own hands and send a caravan to Santa Fe.

Those who shared in the reckless enterprise insisted that their intent was simply to open a merchant trail into New Mexico. True, they admitted, they carried with them proclamations inviting the people of that neighboring province to revolt against their masters and join the Republic of Texas. But, said the Texans, if the citizens of New Mexico declined the invitation, the caravan members would then trade like any merchants and return home in peace.

The story is hard to believe. Two hundred and seventy volunteer soldiers accompanied the caravan. Their leader, Hugh McLeod, was also a general in the Texas army. They had a brass cannon with them. Supposedly this force was to protect the merchants against Indians. But in the entire caravan there were only twenty-five wagons for carrying both trade goods and the supplies needed by the soldiers. In other words, there were very few merchants and they took very little merchandise.

On the other hand, if the expedition was military rather than commercial, it was foolishly planned. Two hundred and seventy soldiers were not enough to invade an enemy province. They could win only with outside help — and that seems to be exactly what they were counting on. Two years before, in the winter of 1838-39, the Pueblo Indians of New Mexico had revolted against the officials in Santa Fe. Governor Manuel Armijo (pronounced *Armee' ho*) had defeated them, but apparently the Texans thought the Pueblos would once again rise in arms to aid an invasion by outsiders.

This was a hope only. The members of the expedition — in Western history it is called the Texas-Santa Fe expedition — did not really know what they would find in New Mexico. Worse still, they did not even know how to get there! No trails ran from Texas to the capital of New Mexico. No guide could be found who knew the land. Hostile Kiowa and Comanche Indians lurked along the way. The season planned for departure was June, so late that the terrible heat of summer was certain to wither the grass and dry the water holes.

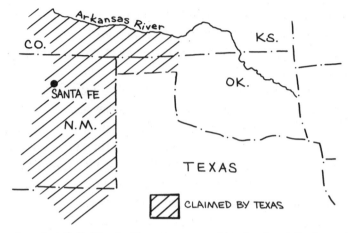

In spite of all this, the Texans went recklessly ahead. In the entire history of the West, there has never been a more ill-judged adventure.

The airline distance to Santa Fe is less than 600 miles. The distance the caravan covered in its wanderings was more than 1300! Wastefully they ate up the beef cattle with which they started, and when buffalo proved harder to find than expected, the men began to suffer from hunger. The rough land drained away their strength. Getting a single wagon up some of the steep, muddy stream banks required the combined efforts of twenty horses and fifty cursing men straining on ropes and against the mired wheels.

In what is now called the Texas Panhandle, great chasms cut the plains. As the men were plodding wearily ahead, unexpected cliffs hundreds of feet deep dropped away almost in front of their toes. Grueling days were spent crossing these terrible gorges — days of heat and thirst, labor and discouragement.

Discipline gave way as the starving men scattered to find grape and plum thickets, to shoot prairie dogs for food, even to try to catch snakes and lizards to eat. Once a roaring prairie fire almost engulfed the wagons. Indians slipping up at night stole horses before the exhausted guards could strike back.

In desperation three men were sent ahead to get help from New Mexico. Meanwhile the caravan broke into two sections. About ninety of the soldiers and twelve of the merchants pushed on in advance with the best of the remaining horses.

This breakup of the caravan made victory easy for Manuel Armijo, the Governor of New Mexico. When the caravan's three messengers reached his capital seeking help, Armijo had them arrested as spies. They escaped from jail but were recaptured. One was killed resisting; the other two were later executed. Armijo then led an army of several hundred militia out to meet the Texans.

The invaders were in no condition to fight as they straggled out of the wilderness. Some did not even have guns to surrender. They were so enfeebled by hunger and hardship that they had thrown their weapons away rather than be burdened with the extra weight.

The wretched captives were assembled in a single column. On foot, without proper food, they were herded through the bitter cold of winter to prison in Mexico City. Several died along the way. Although the survivors were soon released by the Mexican Government, the story of their suffering aroused great excitement and hot indignation not only in Texas but also in the United States.

Texans called for revenge. One wild-eyed individual named Charles Warfield came up with a rash plan for raiding the Santa Fe Trail. Warfield knew the district. He had traveled with the caravans and had trapped in the mountains. It was his belief that he could recruit followers in the frontier towns of Missouri and among the trappers who spent their winters loafing around the trading posts at the foot of the Rockies.

After complicated plotting, it was decided that Warfield would go north to the Santa Fe Trail, gather as many men as he could, and spend the winter of 1842-43 causing trouble in New Mexico. The following spring another force of raiders under a man named Jacob Snively would march north from Texas and join Warfield's outlaws somewhere along the Arkansas River. Together the gangs would attack the 1843 caravans. To avoid trouble with the United States, the raiders proposed to strike only at wagons belonging to Mexican citizens and to do this west of the 100th meridian on territory claimed (without much justice) by the Republic of Texas.

To start the scheme rolling, Warfield rode first to Missouri. There he commissioned a ruffian named John McDaniel to recruit helpers along the frontier. He instructed McDaniel to take his recruits west in the spring and join Warfield and Snively at their rendezvous on the Arkansas River.

To get still more men for the illegal "army," Warfield next hurried to the mountains. There he spent the winter trying to enroll trappers under his leadership. Fewer than two-dozen men joined him. With these desperados Warfield marched into New Mexico to "cause trouble" as planned. Most of it he caused to himself! Near the village of Mora he surprised and defeated a camp of Mexican cavalry. Victory made him careless. The Mexicans counterattacked at night, seized Warfield's unguarded horses, and sent his men fleeing on foot back across Raton Pass.

When the people at Bent's Fort refused to furnish the outlaws with fresh supplies, several of the group deserted. With those who remained, Warfield marched eastward along the trail to his appointed rendezvous with McDaniel and with the other raiders Jacob Snively was bringing up out of Texas.

McDaniel never reached the rendezvous. He had succeeded in recruiting only a dozen or so men. As these outlaws traveled west along the Santa Fe Trail toward Warfield, they encountered a small caravan coming from New Mexico. It belonged to a New Mexican named Antonio José Chávez.

The McDaniel gang attacked Chávez's outfit, robbed him of $11,000 in gold and furs and then began quarreling about whether to kill him. Half of the attackers, refusing to participate in murder, took their share of the booty and withdrew. McDaniel and the others then killed Chávez. Frightened belatedly by what they had done, they fled back toward the east to try to hide themselves in the settlements.

The murder was discovered and reported almost immediately by another party headed toward Missouri. Reaction was swift. Although most United States citizens sympathized with Texas in her quarrel with Mexico, this outrage was too shocking to go unpunished. Members of the McDaniel gang were tracked down and arrested. The leaders were executed and the others sent to prison.

More important, so far as international relations were concerned, the United States learned, through this episode, of the outlaws' plans to attack the trade caravans. Army headquarters immediately ordered Captain Philip St. George Cooke and a troop of cavalry to escort the spring caravan as far as the border. Philip St. George Cooke was famous for his fierce temper and the bushy black beard almost as long as his name.

The Mexican Government had also learned of the outlaws' plans. With 600 militia, Governor Armijo started down the Cimarron end of the trail to meet and protect the caravan. A few unfriendly trappers in Taos watched his army's departure and rushed a warning to Snively's raiders camped near the Arkansas.

By this time, Warfield had joined Snively and was sharing command of the raiders with him. All told, they had about 180 men. Taking half the group with him, Warfield laid an ambush for Armijo and his New Mexicans. The advance guard, many of them Indians whom Armijo had drafted against their will in Taos, walked blindly into the trap and were routed. In panic the survivors fled back to the main army. To Armijo they reported that an overwhelming number of Texans lay ahead. Armijo ordered a retreat. If the caravan approaching his country was to be saved, someone else would have to do it.

That spring was unusually rainy. The heavy mud of the prairies delayed the merchant wagons, twenty-four of which belonged to Americans and thirty-two to Mexicans. As the wet days dragged by without action, Snively's raiders grew impatient. Recklessly they crossed the Arkansas to the north bank.

Snively thought he was west of a line called the 100th meridian, and therefore still inside territory claimed by Texas. But even if he were on United States ground he anticipated no trouble with Captain Cooke. Weren't the Texans and Americans friends?

Cooke himself was not sure whose territory he was on. And he was a very good friend of Texans. But not of outlaws. As the two forces drew near each other, he deployed his men. Suddenly the raiders realized that they were surrounded. His eyes severe and icy above his long beard, Cooke ordered Snively to have the raiders throw down their arms.

Snively began a furious protest. It dwindled as Cooke's troopers thumbed back the hammers of their guns. Glumly the Texan gave the necessary order. His men tossed their rifles into a heap, and the caravan rolled on unmolested.

In spite of this episode, relations between the United States and Mexico grew more and more strained. The Republic of Texas wanted to enter the American commonwealth as a state. Most Americans favored the move. But the Mexican Government angrily declared that any such happening would mean war between their country and the United States.

While diplomats argued, the American army quietly made preparations. During the summer of 1845 three expeditions were sent out to explore the western lands. Of the three, the most important to the future of the Santa Fe Trail was one led by Colonel Stephen Watts Kearny.

After marching westward into Wyoming, Kearny turned south to Bent's Fort on the Arkansas. He could not cross the river onto Mexican soil. But there were other ways of getting information about the enemy's strength in the Southwest. While his soldiers wandered about the fort staring at the Indians, Colonel Kearny met with the Bents and Céran St. Vrain in the owners' elaborate apartment on top of the adobe battlements. From these men the Colonel learned vital information about the state of affairs in New Mexico.

If war came — and everyone was sure it would — Stephen Kearny's Army of the West would be ready.

9

Army on the Trail

*T*he war came in May, 1846. Although its decisive battles would be fought in Old Mexico, Santa Fe and the cities of California were too important to be overlooked. At once Stephen Watts Kearny was ordered to move against New Mexico with an army of 1700 volunteers. That conquest completed, he was to cross the deserts to California if conditions justified.

Organizing 1700 raw recruits into an efficient army and marching them on foot across 800 miles of barren plains promised to be a staggering job. Moreover, time was short. Travelers coming east along the trail brought rumors that the Mexicans were sending reinforcements from the south. With their reinforcements the enemy hoped to slice in behind Kearny's army, cut the Americans off from their supplies, and then defeat the invaders at their leisure — or so the rumors said.

To prevent this, Kearny hoped to reach and attack New Mexico before the Mexicans could put their own plans into execution. As a rendezvous point for gathering his forces, the Colonel selected Bent's Fort on the Arkansas River, the border between the two countries.

But he had not a day to spare. It was late May already and he wanted to reach the fort before the end of July.

Fortunately for Kearny, the volunteers who poured into Fort Leavenworth in eastern Kansas to join the Army of the West were husky young men from the frontier farms. Outdoor work in all kinds of weather had put them in first-class physical condition. To help train them, Kearny had the plains-toughened dragoons he had taken west the previous summer and experienced officers like Philip St. George Cooke.

As the new recruits were being taught the first rudiments of discipline, Kearny shifted his attention to the civilian traders. Scores of them had guessed that war was coming and that the price of goods in Santa Fe would soar sky-high as soon as the Trail was closed by the hostilities. Accordingly more than 400 wagons had been fitted out to hurry west in advance of the army. It was twice as many vehicles as ever before had gone to Santa Fe.

Kearny did not want these wagons to reach New Mexico ahead of him. Many of them, especially those belonging to Mexican proprietors, would carry useful supplies and information to the enemy. Also, if a battle had to be fought in Santa Fe, the American proprietors would be in the way. They would expect their lives and property to be protected, yet in the fury of conflict this might not be possible.

As soon as the official declaration of war reached Kearny he sent out cavalry to stop the traders, particularly one train of Mexican wagons suspected of carrying powder and lead to Governor Armijo. The Mexicans, however, had a long start. By putting extra teams on their wagons, a few of them managed to cross the border to the Cimarron before the dragoons could overtake them. The bulk of the merchants were stopped, nevertheless, as they lumbered along the Arkansas and were ordered to go to Bent's Fort and wait for the army there.

Behind the traders came ragged columns of army supply wagons loaded with uniforms, food, medicine, guns — all the equipment that 1700 men might need. Beside the wagons plodded herds of beef cattle to make up for the buffalo which were certain to be frightened away from the trail by the passage of so much traffic.

The military wagon trains were in miserable shape. Traders had taken over most of the good teams, sound vehicles, and experienced workers on the frontier. The result was chaos. The army's green livestock stampeded; wagons broke down; drivers took fright at imaginary Indian attacks and ran away, leaving their equipment stranded. Not the least amazing part of the advance on the West was the way the quartermasters overcame one disaster after another and kept the soldiers supplied with food and clothing as they toiled toward New Mexico.

The recruits were issued arms and sent marching down the Santa Fe Trail almost before they knew how to form into squads. Kearny believed the men could be trained as they moved. Some of his officers were aghast, but the experiment worked. The grim conditions of the Trail imposed discipline even on the unruly farmhands. Otherwise they could hardly have survived.

The summer heat was terrible. Dust fogged in choking clouds. Maddening swarms of gnats settled in the corners of the men's eyes and in their nostrils. Their feet blistered; their legs swelled. They were always thirsty, yet they soon learned that if they drank the foul water of the buffalo wallows, it would bring on cramps more painful than their parched throats.

The sick and weak collapsed and were put into ambulance wagons. Though loudly complaining, as soldiers always do, the strong began to take pride in their ability to keep going. They learned to obey orders and to march in better formation. They stepped out with

longer strides. The distances they covered in a day increased from fifteen miles to twenty, to twenty-five. Triumphantly they discovered that they were actually out-walking the cavalry horses and reached each night's camp ground ahead of the leg-weary beasts.

Late in July the huge, disjointed mixture of traders, freighters, cavalry, and infantry rolled up to Bent's Fort. They overwhelmed the establishment. They turned its spare rooms into hospitals for the sick; they stood in noisy lines at the shops to repair gear and weapons and to shoe their animals. They clamored in the store to buy goods the fort did not possess. Their 20,000 head of mules, oxen, and horses grazed for miles along the valley bottom. White wagon tops and white tents shone in the sun as far as the eye could reach.

Kearny, who wanted to avoid bloodshed if possible, sent messengers from the fort with proclamations to the people of New Mexico. These proclamations promised that if the enemy made no resistance, no damage would be done and the native customs would be respected. Resistance had to be prepared for, however. Although the rumor about Mexican reinforcements from the south had proved false, new alarms said that Governor Armijo had mustered a large army of New Mexicans and Pueblo Indians and was preparing to give battle somewhere in the mountains between Bent's Fort and Santa Fe.

The rough country contained many spots where a disastrous ambush could be laid. To make sure that the American troops fell into no such trap, William Bent was sent ahead with a company of mountain men to scout the way. Reformed and resupplied, the soldiers followed the scouts across the Arkansas River into the most difficult country they had yet encountered. Temperatures along Timpas Creek boiled up above one hundred degrees. Alkali dust made eyes and throats raw with pain. The water holes, too small for so many thirsty drinkers, were spoiled by the cavalry horses for the infanty who followed.

The road which the Bents long ago had built through Raton Pass was rough at best. The passage of vast quantities of the army's freight made it worse. At one point just beyond the summit, men had to detach the tangled teams from some of the vehicles and by hand boost the groaning wagons over the boulders and along the dizzy ledges.

Anywhere along the line the unwieldy army might have broken down. But somehow Kearny kept the tired men pushing ahead. They met no resistance. Though Armijo had started to build fortifications in a pass near Santa Fe, he fled from the rapidly approaching Americans. There are reasons for believing he had been bribed by United States agents to do this. If so, many lives were saved; and in the middle of August, Kearny's Army of the West entered the capital of New Mexico without firing a shot.

Not long after the occupation, American reinforcements marched into New Mexico along the Cimarron branch of the Santa Fe Trail. Kearny, who recently had been promoted to the rank of General, did not think the additional men were needed. The residents of New Mexico seemed resigned to the conquest. Even the Indians of the mountains had promised to sign treaties of peace. Accordingly, Kearny decided to take some of the newly arrived soldiers to California with his own troops. The remainder he ordered south to join the invasion of Old Mexico. Only a handful of men were left behind to garrison Santa Fe. Many outlying towns like Taos received no troops whatsoever.

Such weakness was, of course, an invitation to trouble. Plotting began as soon as Kearny was out of sight. The plot was foiled when a servant girl of one of the conspirators learned of the plan and ran with a warning to friends of the Americans. Quickly the word was passed on to the man whom Kearny had appointed Governor of the new territory — Charles Bent.

Thanks to the early discovery, Charles quickly checked the would-be revolution — completely, he thought. In January, 1847, unaware that trouble still smoldered, he decided to go home to Taos for a brief rest with his beautiful Mexican wife Ignacia and their three children. Kit Carson's wife, Josefa, a sister of Ignacia's, was also living in the Bent home that winter, for Kit was away in California.

Charles knew there were no troops in Taos, but he had lived in the town so long and had so many friends there that he could not imagine danger. Certain rebel leaders decided, however, that this was their chance. They intended to assassinate the American governor.

They marshaled their forces and worked the men into a frenzy during the night of January 18. At dawn on the 19th, the excited, howling mob attacked Charles's home.

He was the only man in the house. He had weapons, but decided not to use them, fearing that bloodshed would so madden the attackers that they would harm his and Kit's wives and the children. Stepping unarmed to the door, he tried to pacify the Mexicans and Indians with words. They shouted him down. A bow twanged, the mob surged forward. Charles Bent, for nearly twenty years the most familiar figure on the Santa Fe Trail, dropped dead.

His bravery saved his family. The rebels did not harm them. But nearly every other American or American sympathizer in Taos was slain. One named Charles Towne escaped, and carried word of the tragedy across seventy miles of snowy trail to Santa Fe.

The commander in Santa Fe, Colonel Sterling Price, had less than three hundred men available for fighting. To secure additional strength he turned to Céran St. Vrain. Quickly Céran assembled sixty-five trappers and merchants who had known and loved the murdered Governor. In bitter cold weather the tiny force of 353 men started north. Fifteen hundred Mexicans and Indians massed to meet them.

The Americans were disciplined and well armed; the rebels were not. The difference was crucial. In two sharp battles the enemy were defeated. Completely disorganized, they fled for refuge to the sprawling Indian pueblo a few miles beyond Taos. There they fortified themselves behind the thick adobe walls of the pueblo's windowless church. The Americans marched against the building. From loopholes high in the walls, the rebels defended themselves. Charging through the hail of bullets and arrows, volunteers managed to reach one wall and flatten against it, too close under the loopholes for the rebel fire to reach them. With axes and crowbars they hacked a small hole through the adobe and tossed in grenades. Then a cannon was run up. Its round shot battered the hole still larger. Shouting infantrymen swarmed into the building, and soon the battle was over.

Even before this, Kearny's forces had reached California to help complete the conquest of that far territory. Other American troops invading Old Mexico won victory after victory, and soon the defeated country was suing for peace. In the treaty which ended the war, all of the Southwest passed into the hands of the victors, and the United States stretched unbroken from coast to coast.

10

Tragic Years

*E*ven while the rebels were being crushed at Taos, Indian war drums were beginning to throb across the plains. The Indians had many grievances. For years the buffalo herds had been shrinking in size. Partly it was the fault of the Indians themselves, who each winter killed more and more of the shaggy beasts in order to sell their hides at the trading posts; but much of the loss was due to American hunters. After the outbreak of the war with Mexico the slaughter of buffalo by the whites increased so markedly that the Indians were roused to fury.

Every one of the thousands of soldiers and teamsters flowing west along the Santa Fe Trail was armed, and nearly every one of them took an excited delight in shooting at the huge animals whether they needed meat or not. Furthermore, the indiscriminate killings and the traffic frightened the herds away from the Trail and interrupted the seasonal migrations.

To the Indians this disappearance of game from their favorite hunting grounds was serious. The red men lost not only their main article of commerce but also their chief supply of food, clothing, and skins for making tepees.

There were other wrongs as well. Almost the only trees in the high, dry plains were groves of gnarled cottonwoods straggling along the streambanks. The Indians used these groves for shade in summer and shelter in winter. Thriftily they saved every dry twig for firewood. When snow covered the grass, they could keep their ponies alive by feeding the animals tender bark stripped from the small limbs. Trees were also important to the Indians because of their custom of placing the bodies of their dead on platforms across the high branches, instead of burying them.

White men seldom understood how important the scrawny groves were to the Indians. Soldiers and freighters carelessly chopped down the trees when in need of wood for any purpose — and sometimes for no other reason than just to be chopping. They built campfires so big they could not sit up close to them the way the Indians did; then they would march away from enough smoldering wood to have kept a tepee warm for a week. But the worst thing of all was the way souvenir hunters wantonly robbed the Indian tree graves of curios.

Intensifying these reasons for war was the Plains Indian's in-grained love of battle. Boys were brought up to believe that the highest goal in life was to be a successful warrior. A girl's dreams centered on marrying a brave whose triumphs in arms would bring fame to his family. When Americans and Mexicans took to fighting each other, the young warriors itched for action of their own, especially when they contemplated the rich booty moving along the trail.

Never before had the Indians seen so many wagons driven by in-experienced teamsters or so many fat horses and mules in the charge of careless herders. The risk of seizing these prizes seemed slight. The whites were concentrating on each other. They could not, or so the chiefs believed, muster additional forces for battling the Indians.

Impelled by all these things, the Indians in 1847 launched a series of hit-and-run attacks whose tragic end they could not foresee. Only the Cheyennes and the Arapahos held back, largely because of their friendship for the Bents. All the others struck — the Pawnees near the eastern end of the Santa Fe Trail, the Comanches and Kiowas along the Cimarron, the Utes and Jicarilla Apaches in the western mountains.

It was not a unified war, but rather a series of independent raids. At first the attacks were dramatically successful. Wild victory dances swirled through smoky firelight in the villages as the war parties came home with their plunder. During the first few months of the war, the various Indian attacks netted more than 6000 head of the white man's livestock. Warriors robbed and destroyed 330 wagons — six times as many as had been in the train which Captain Cooke had saved from Snively's and Warfield's raiders from Texas. Forty-seven Americans were slain — nearly nine times as many as had been killed by Indians in the previous forty years since Zebulon Pike had found his way to the forbidden city of Santa Fe.

Such losses would not be tolerated. Even before the troops were back from the Mexican War, another five companies of volunteers were raised in Missouri and placed in command of Lieutenant Colonel William Gilpin.

In the fall of 1847 Gilpin started west. Half his troops he left in Kansas to build a fort. With the other half he continued up the Arkansas River a short distance beyond Bent's Fort. There winter caught him and he had to settle down in a cold, hungry bivouac. But as soon as spring came, he was on the move again, down the Cimarron and back to the Arkansas.

Wherever he could bring the Indians to bay, he fought them. The tribes paid grievously for their earlier successes. At least 250 warriors from the various tribes died in battle. The survivors refused to surrender, however. Widows and daughters of the slain men wailed among the tepees, begging their war councils to seek revenge. As soon as Gilpin's troops had passed on beyond reach, the Indians struck once more at the Trail. So dangerous did the way become that even as experienced an Indian fighter as Kit Carson would not travel it. Instead, he went east in the summer of 1848 by a long roundabout swing through Nebraska.

The summer's fighting convinced Gilpin that the only way to handle the situation was to build several forts in the Indian country and to station cavalry in them. At the first sign of trouble the troops could ride out with enough show of strength to keep the Indians in awe. He himself had built one such fort in Kansas, and now he recommended that the Army buy another — Bent's Fort on the Arkansas River.

The United States Army offered William Bent $12,000 for the historic post. William did not think it was enough. He was in a gloomy frame of mind that year of 1849. Of the four brothers who had followed the Santa Fe Trail to the West, he alone remained. Robert had been killed by Comanches; Charles had been murdered during the revolt in Taos; shortly after the war, George had been taken mortally sick at the fort and had died in spite of everything that William could do. At about the same time William's Cheyenne Indian wife, Owl Woman, died after giving birth to their fourth child, a boy whom the grief-stricken father named Charles.

Added to these personal sorrows were business worries. Céran St. Vrain, prospering in New Mexico, was no longer interested in continuing the Indian trade. William would have to go ahead alone, and make radical changes in the process. Because of the wars, the tribes had shifted their hunting grounds, and the fort's location was no longer as desirable as it had been. The Cheyennes and Arapahos now preferred to gather at the Big Timbers, a grove of cottonwoods forty miles down the Arkansas to the east.

William decided to follow them. But he could not bear to let the fort where he had spent the best years of his life fall into the hands of strangers, either Indians or the Army. On impulse he removed the goods, rolled kegs of gunpowder into some of the rooms, and set the fuses afire. With a great roar large sections of the most famous post in the Southwest — a post William Bent himself had created a quarter of a century before — went up in smoke.

That same year, 1849, thousands upon thousands of Forty-niners were pouring west toward the newly discovered gold fields in California. Though most of the emigrants used the Overland Trail to the north, the Santa Fe trace received a considerable share. Most of the hurrying travelers did not understand the plains and were incapable of defending themselves. If an outbreak of cholera had not swept through the tribes that summer, attacks on the whites might have been worse. As it was, however, hundreds of Indians died during the epidemic. Those who were spared were so frightened by the mysterious disease that for the time being they ceased their raids.

Change piled on change. In the Big Timbers, William Bent built in 1853 a huge stone post called Bent's New Fort. That same year government surveyors, passed up the Arkansas River, looking for a possible route a railroad could follow to the Pacific. Other parties of engineers were examining other routes across the southern, central, and northern parts of the country. The Indians watched the different groups curiously, not realizing that if steel rails ever followed the stakes which the white men were driving into the prairie sod, the old life would be forever ended.

The whites themselves delayed the laying of the rails with their own quarrels. The Civil War was fast approaching. Neither the North nor the South wanted its opponent strengthened by a railroad linking it to the rich, vigorous new state of California. Each route that was proposed in Congress was violently attacked by partisans from other sections of the country, and as a result no railroad was built then.

Even without the rails, nevertheless, the Indians of the plains were soon faced with an overwhelming threat to their ancient homes. In 1859, ten years after the gold rush to California, there was another stampede to Colorado. The Rockies of Colorado were relatively near the advancing frontier. A trip across the plains now seemed little more than a picnic. Larger hordes of white settlers than ever before swarmed across the buffalo ranges. At the foot of the mountains, on a favorite camping ground of the Arapahos, the city of Denver took shape. Other towns appeared north and south along the eastern base of the foothills.

To protect these travelers the Army at last erected a string of forts along all the main trails, including the road to Santa Fe. William Bent rented his new fort to the government and withdrew to a ranch at the mouth of the Purgatoire River.

Before the Army could complete its post at Bent's stone building, a new white man's conflict broke out. This was the Civil War. A Confederate force from Texas invaded New Mexico and marched up the Rio Grande. After defeating the Union Army that tried to stop them at Valverde, the Southerners seized Santa Fe.

The triumphant Rebels now plotted to conquer the entire Southwest. Agents were sent among the restless Indians in an effort to persuade them to attack Union forts and supply trains along the Santa Fe Trail. The Indians held back, however. The Comanches did not wish to become allies of their ancient enemies, the Texans, and William Bent persuaded the Cheyennes and Arapahos to keep the peace with white men that they had never broken.

This failure of the Indians to take to the warpath gave Colorado volunteers a chance to hurry to the aid of the remnants of the Union Army in New Mexico. The combined forces caught the Confederate invaders in a pass near Santa Fe, destroyed their supply wagons, and drove them back toward Texas.

Two years later the Indians might not have been so obliging. By then the Sioux had gone on the warpath and, in spite of William Bent, some of the Cheyennes, outraged by the loss of their buffalo grounds, joined them. Raids by the two tribes spread so far and grew so terrible that for months the new city of Denver did not receive a pound of supplies from the East.

Angry and frightened, the Colorado troops turned their guns against the Indians. Colonel Chivington, the officer who had led the volunteers against the Confederates in New Mexico, treacherously attacked a peaceful Cheyenne village on Sand Creek, not far from the Santa Fe Trail. As many women and children as warriors were killed by the whites during the brutal fight. In revengeful fury, the full Cheyenne and Arapaho tribes then joined the general war. Two of William Bent's half-Indian sons went with the red men into battle against their father's people.

It was a hopeless effort. As soon as the Civil War ended, overwhelming numbers of trained white soldiers were rushed west. The defeated tribes one by one reluctantly signed peace treaties and let themselves be moved, not always without bloodshed, onto reservations.

By 1868 all but the tag ends of the tragic war were over. In that same year residents of Topeka, Kansas, decided that times were ripe to start building a railroad along the trail to Santa Fe.

11

Steel Wheels Roll

*I*n their own way the railroad builders were as rugged as the teamsters whom they drove out of business. With no more protection than rifles and wits, surveyors ranged ahead of the work crews to find the route. Following their stakes came the graders. They had no machinery. They tore raw scars through the thick, matted sod with heavy breaking plows hitched behind long teams of mules. They dug deep cuts through the hills with picks and shovels. They cleaned out the dirt with horse-drawn scrapers, then used the same scrapers for heaping up long dikes of earth in the fills.

Behind them came brawny gangs of roustabouts laying heavy bridge timbers and steel rails, bolting on fish plates and driving spikes. Good weather or foul, they drove the gleaming track steadily on and on. Since they were always moving, they could have none of the comforts of a stationary camp. They slept in huge tents that by dint of tight crowding held as many as a hundred men. Their beds were canvas packed with straw, or perhaps just pine boards elevated enough to keep them out of the dust and mud. They ate from rough tables in another long tent or in a shack hastily nailed together out of scrap lumber. Day after day their food was the same: beans, salt pork, soggy bread, molasses. On Sunday there might be a treat — pie made from dried fruit.

The Union Pacific was the first of the railroads to build west across the plains, but it was too far north to affect the Santa Fe Trail. Next, and farther to the south, the Kansas Pacific Railroad started toward Denver in the late 1860's. The route was close enough to the Santa Fe Trail that the great wagon caravans turned north to meet the advancing railhead. The shift marked the beginning of the end of the old days. At Council Grove, where once the merchants had paused to elect their captains, the deep wagon ruts lay empty. As one Kansas newspaper described the change: "The shriek of the iron horse has silenced the lowing of the panting ox, and the old Trail looks desolate."

Then, to change completely the appearance of the land, the Atchison, Topeka, and Santa Fe Railroad started west. Short of money, the builders moved slowly at first. Soon, however, the track laying became a race against time. In order for the company to obtain the land grants which the government was giving it as an aid in financing the construction, the rails had to reach the Colorado border by January 1, 1873. On May 1, 1872, the iron was still 271 miles short of the goal. To succeed, the laborers would have to put down through the wilderness a mile of track each and every day.

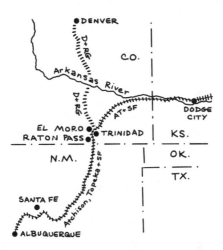

More money was borrowed, more workers hired, more livestock purchased, more construction camps built. Singing, brawling, fighting the weather and each other, the thousands of men drove westward through the drought of summer into the icy gales of winter. On December 28, 1872, three days ahead of the deadline, they reached the border.

Behind them came changes such as William Becknell and William Bent could never have believed. Raw towns sprang up on the old campgrounds. Wildest of them all and forever a part of our pioneer history was Dodge City. Nicknamed the "Queen of the Cowtowns," Dodge City was located near the spot where Captain Philip St. George Cooke had disarmed Snively's raiders from Texas. But now Texans — and their cattle — were more welcome.

After the Civil War, cattle were about the only thing in the huge southern state that was worth money — if the cattle could be sent to market in the North. One possibility was to drive the longhorns to the new railroads and then ship the animals in freight cars to the meat-packing plants in Chicago.

At first the trail drivers took their herds to Abilene and Hays City on the Kansas Pacific Railroad; but after the Santa Fe pushed up the Arkansas River farther south, Dodge City captured the trade. It was a rough, wide-open town. Fourteen men were murdered during the first year of its existence, but finally the better citizens decided to drive the criminal element out. As peace officer they selected Bat Masterson, who once had worked as a grader for the Santa Fe and whose brother was killed by outlaws right on the railroad tracks themselves. Gradually, knowing he had the support of the town behind him, Masterson restored order.

Dodge City was never a gentle town, however. Its business came not only from cowboys eager to spend their wages after the dangerous drive from Texas, but also from an equally rough group, the buffalo hunters.

In the early days of the Trail, white men had left the preparation of buffalo robes to the Indians. But with the approach of the railroad, hides could easily be brought to the freight yards, loaded onto the trains, and shipped east to quick profits. The result was probably the biggest slaughter of game in history.

In 1874 nearly half a million buffalo hides were shipped from Dodge City alone. One famous hunter, Brick Bond, was said to have killed 6000 buffalo in two months. Tom Nickerson slew 140 in forty minutes. After the terrible slaughter was over, settlers picked ton upon ton of bleaching bones off the prairies and shipped them east to fertilizer factories. Homesteaders near Granada, Colorado, for instance, stacked up beside the railroad tracks an enormous bone pile twelve feet high, twelve feet wide, and half a mile long!

Within a few years the buffalo herds had vanished. The prairies opened for the grazing of cattle and for the farms of immigrants. To increase its traffic, the Santa Fe, like all railroads, sent agents to Europe to encourage settlers to come to America. By the thousands the im-

migrants crossed the ocean to the rich promises of the West. The land that once the merchant caravans had regarded as empty wilderness to be crossed as quickly as possible, now furnished homesites for a growing nation.

In 1875 the Santa Fe Railroad reached up the Arkansas River past Bent's Old Fort. The building's damaged walls had been repaired, and for years the structure had served as a stage station on the run from Denver to Santa Fe. But after the railroad came, the fort was again abandoned. Farmers packed away its adobe bricks for building barns and corrals. Slowly under the rain and snow of the years, the last traces of the once-famous post crumbled back into the earth.

A few miles west of the fort the town of La Junta took shape. This was near the crossing where the wagon trains of Bent, St. Vrain & Company once had forded the river and had struck toward Raton Pass. The Santa Fe Railroad turned in the same direction, aiming for the same opening into New Mexico.

The Santa Fe's move was immediately challenged by a vigorous Colorado railway called the Denver & Rio Grande Railroad. As its name suggests, the Denver & Rio Grande intended to build south to the Mexican border. It was also building west into the rich mining camps of the Rockies, and its managers knew that the Santa Fe line was a threat to both plans. Therefore the Denver & Rio Grande wanted to seize Raton Pass ahead of its rival, for the narrow approaches to the gap would accommodate only one roadbed. Whichever company started construction first would be the one to win the prize.

The Denver & Rio Grande seemed to have the advantage. Its tracks already reached to the foot of the pass at a station called El Moro. El Moro was a railroad town pure and simple. The Denver & Rio Grande owned every foot of land in the vicinity and had put its depot at El Moro in hope of attracting settlers to whom it could sell building lots. The action enraged the already established town of Trinidad, four miles away. Merchants in Trinidad felt that their business was deliberately being ruined for the benefit of the rival town. As a result, Trinidad citizens were eager to counter the move by attracting the Santa Fe Railroad to their city.

In 1876 the Santa Fe did not have enough money to start expensive construction work in the mountains. Fully aware of the road's poverty, officials of the Denver & Rio Grande decided there was no hurry to start their own track toward the pass. Their company was poor, too, and they wanted to spend what funds they had completing their own lines to the gold and silver camps.

They did decide, however, to survey a roadbed through Raton Pass. With the survey completed they would be ready to start construction at once, if by any chance the Santa Fe Railroad showed signs of beginning to move. The first sign, of course, would be a survey of the pass by Santa Fe engineers. Such activity would be easy to detect in plenty of time — or so the Denver & Rio Grande people thought.

In the summer of 1876, the year Colorado became a state, Denver & Rio Grande engineers went to work in the pass. As they pushed higher among the cliffs and pine trees, they kept meeting sheep herded by a lazy-seeming man wearing the tall sombrero and serape of a poor Mexican. They paid no attention to him. Why bother about a sheepherder?

Actually the man was Raymond Morley, an engineer for the Santa Fe. Morley watched every move the rivals made. He also surveyed, right under their noses, a route for the Santa Fe Railroad. His company, too, would be ready to move as soon as funds were available.

Another person whom the Denver & Rio Grande people ignored was Uncle Dick Wootton, a grizzled old trapper who lived on the Colorado side of the pass. Why bother about trappers any more than about sheepherders?

Morley was wiser. Carefully, he cultivated Uncle Dick's friendship. In their association the old and the new West joined hands.

Once Dick Wootton had worked at Bent's Fort as an Indian trader and buffalo hunter. He had trapped through the mountains as far away as Oregon. He had driven sheep to the gold fields in California and had run huge ox-drawn freight trains down the old Trail from Independence to Santa Fe. After the Civil War he had decided that what Raton Pass needed was a road that did not shake wagons half to pieces.

Uncle Dick built the road himself, twenty-seven hard miles of it. He charged the people who used it tolls. He also built a little log store and hotel in the pass where travelers could stay. A railroad would ruin his business, but he knew that progress could not be stopped. The thing that made him angry was not railroading in general, but one railroad in particular — the Denver & Rio Grande. He did not like the way his friends in Trinidad had been treated. He liked his own treatment even less. Who did the Denver & Rio Grande surveyors think they were, anyway, ignoring him and his toll road as if they did not exist?

Raymond Morley was different. He liked to sit around the fire in Uncle Dick's hotel and listen to stories of the old days. That was the kind of railroader a man did not mind helping.

Two years passed. Then, in February of 1878, the Santa Fe construction engineers, Raymond Morley included, received orders to take crews into Raton Pass and start work. The Denver & Rio Grande learned of the plan at once, for their telegraph lines joined the Santa Fe's in Pueblo and their operators had discovered how to decode Santa Fe messages. Orders were flashed out for Denver & Rio Grande engineers to start grading ahead of the Santa Fe.

The engineers of both companies planned to hire the necessary construction workers at the foot of the pass, the Denver & Rio Grande in El Moro, the Santa Fe in Trinidad. By chance both groups of engineers rode the same train to El Moro. But the Santa Fe men saw their rivals without being recognized themselves.

Haste was vital. The first crew at work in the pass would win. Morley persuaded his companions not to spend time hiring men in Trinidad. Instead, they rented a buggy at the livery stable and galloped through the freezing night to Uncle Dick Wootton's hotel.

It was a Saturday night. Morley knew that young people from Trinidad often went to the hotel to dance, and that freighters frequently stopped there en route to New Mexico. If they were there tonight . . . .

They were. Swiftly Morley explained the situation. With Uncle Dick in the lead, every man on the place went whooping out into the cold, seized the lanterns and tools which the old trapper had provided, and went vigorously to work. When the Denver & Rio Grande crew panted into sight a few hours later, the race was over. The Santa Fe had won.

To reduce the steep grades in the pass, a tunnel was surveyed several hundred feet below the summit. Miners began boring from both ends. In order that supply trains could reach the tunnel's farther end, a steep temporary track was laid over the top of the pass. In January, 1879, the first engine, named *Uncle Dick*, toiled to the summit.

There it paused for a brief ceremony. The men who stepped down from the train knew that they were making history. They were standing with an iron horse where more than half a century before William Becknell had stood beside his weary pack mules; where the Bent brothers had come with the first wagons; where Kearny's Army of the West had marched.

Now steel rails were reaching across to bind the nation into a still tighter whole, to complete a long story of hardship and hope, bloodshed and bravery that had begun seventy-two years earlier when Zebulon Pike first ventured into this bright land.

A FEW MORE BOOKS TO READ

Some of the best books about the Santa Fe Trail were written by people who actually traveled the famous route. Most of these books are still in print and can be found in bookstores and libraries.

In LAND OF ENCHANTMENT Marian Sloan Russell tells of five Trail crossings she and her older brother Will made with their widowed mother. Marian was only seven years old on the first trip she made across the prairies.

Lewis Garrard was a teen-ager in 1846 when he traveled west with a wagon train. He was at Bent's Fort when word arrived of the murder of Territorial Governor Charles Bent and was part of a would-be rescue party that rode across the mountains to Taos. He wrote of his adventures in WAH-TO-YAH AND THE TAOS TRAIL.

Earlier in 1846 Susan Shelby, the eighteen-year-old daughter of a well-to-do family in Independence, Missouri, had married Samuel Magoffin, a Santa Fe trader. She traveled west with the caravan of 1846, accompanied by the Army of the West on its way to conquer New Mexico. DOWN THE SANTA FE TRAIL AND INTO MEXICO is Susan Shelby Magoffin's Trail diary.

Since its publication in 1844 until today, Josiah Gregg's book COMMERCE OF THE PRAIRIES has been read by everyone seriously interested in the Santa Fe Trail. This famous book tells of ten years' trading experience along the Trail, starting in 1831. It is full of information about the landscape, the customs of the Indians and New Mexicans, and the operation of wagon trains.

A collection of several exciting excerpts from Trail accounts has been assembled by historian Marc Simmons in ON THE SANTA FE TRAIL. Simmons has also written a very informative guide to the Santa Fe Trail for modern travelers entitled FOLLOWING THE SANTA FE TRAIL. No one should set out on a trip across the old Trail route without this book in the car. In addition, he has written personal reflections on the Santa Fe Trail to accompany a beautiful photographic study of modern Trail relics by Joan Myers entitled ALONG THE SANTA FE TRAIL.

THE SANTA FE TRAIL, the National Park Service Historic Sites Survey, by William E. Brown provides a thorough history of the Trail along with a catalog of surviving remnants of the old trace.

WAGON TRACKS, the newsletter of Santa Fe Trail Association, is a fine source of information about all Santa Fe Trail topics — new publications and discoveries; celebrations, festivals, meetings and symposiums. You may want to join. For information write:

Santa Fe Trail Association
P.O. Box 1
Woodston, KS 67675

INDEX

Animas River   32, 57
Arkansas River   19, 32, 35, 36, 40, 41, 43, 45, 52, 56, 58, 73, 79, 81, 88, 97
Armijo, Gov. Manuel   71, 73, 75, 76, 79, 81, 82
Atchison, Topeka, and Santa Fe Railroad   95

Baird, James   36, 40
Becknell, William   32-37, 57
Bent, Charles   41-48, 50-53, 55-59, 60, 82-83, 88
Bent, George   56, 60, 88
Bent, Ignacia   82
Bent, Robert   56, 60, 62, 88
Bent, William   40, 44, 45, 55-59, 60, 81, 88-89, 91, 92
Bent, St. Vrain & Co.   46, 47, 50, 53, 63
Bent's Fort   59-60, 74, 78-79, 81, 88-89
Bent's New Fort   89
Big Timbers   89
Bond, Brick   96
Buffalo   85, 96

California   78, 84, 90
Canadian River   53, 56
Carson, Josefa   82
Carson, Kit   37, 45, 60, 82, 88
Chaguanosos   69
Chambers, Samuel   36, 40
Chávez, Antonio José   74
Chihuahua   27, 28, 30, 36, 63, 64, 66
Chivington, Colonel   92
Chouteau, Auguste   30, 31
Cimarron River   35, 39, 45, 53, 61, 76, 88
Civil War   90, 91
Colorado   30, 90
Continental Divide   21
Cooke, Capt. Philip St. George   75, 77, 79, 95

Cooper brothers   34
Cottonwood trees   86
Council Grove   49-50, 51, 95

Dead Man's Journey, 65
De Mun, Jules   30-31
Denver & Rio Grande Railroad   97-98, 99, 100
Deserts   35, 67
Dodge City   35, 95-96

El Moro   98, 100
El Paso   64, 66
Escalante   67

Fort Leavenworth   79
Forty-niners   89
Fowler, Jacob   32
Franklin, Missouri   34, 42

Gila River   55, 67
Gilpin, Lt. Col. William   88
Glenn, Hugh   32-33

Houston, Sam   70

Independence, Missouri   42
Indians   17-18, 38, 39, 43-44, 72, 82, 85-88, 89, 91
    Apache   38, 64
    Arapaho   56, 61, 87, 89, 91
    Cheyenne   56, 58, 61, 87, 89, 91
    Comanche   32, 40, 53, 56, 62, 64, 71, 87, 91
    Delaware   50
    Jicarilla   87
    Kiowa   87
    Navajo   38, 39
    Pawnee   18, 19, 61, 87
    Pueblo   39, 71, 81
    Sioux   91
    Ute   87

Kansas Pacific Railroad   94, 96
Kearny, Col. Stephen Watts   77-82

La Junta   58, 97
Las Animas   58
LaLande   16
Los Médanos   66
Louisiana Purchase   15

McDaniel, John   73-75
McKnight, John   32, 33
McKnight, Robert   32, 33
McLeod, Hugh   71
McNees   39
Masterson, Bat   96
Means, John   40
Mora   74
Morley, Raymond   98-99, 100
Mules   48, 68-69
Munroe   39

Neosho River   49
Nickerson, Tom   96

Oklahoma   32
Old Spanish Trail   67
Overland Trail   89
Oxen   48, 52, 54

Pawnee Rock   52
Picketwire River   32, 57
Pike, Albert   51, 53
Pike, Lt. Zebulon Montgomery, expedition of   15-23
Pikes Peak   19
Price, Col. Sterling   83
Purgatoire River   32, 57, 91

Railroad   89-90, 93-101
Raton Pass   32, 35, 57, 60, 61, 74, 81, 98, 99, 100
Riley, Maj. Bennett   42, 43, 44, 48
Rio Grande   21, 24, 64, 65
Robinson, John   15-16, 19-20, 22, 28

St. Vrain, Céran   45, 47, 56, 58, 60, 77, 83, 89
San Jacinto   70

Sangre de Cristo Mountains   20, 54
Santa Fe   22, 24-26, 34, 38, 53, 56, 63, 66, 69, 71, 78, 82, 83, 91
Santa Fe Railroad   95-101
Smith, Jedediah   53
Snively, Jacob   73, 74, 76, 77
Sublette, William   53

Taos   36, 38, 53, 58, 70, 76, 82-83
Texas   18, 69, 77
Texas-Santa Fe expedition   71
Timpas Creek   81
Topeka   92
Towne, Charles   83
Trinidad, Colorado   57, 98, 100

Union Pacific Railroad   94
Utah   67

Valverde   91
Veracruz   28

Waldo brothers   42
Warfield, Charles   73-76
Wildlife   52
Wilkinson, General   16
Wolfskill, William   67
Wootton, Uncle Dick   99, 100